# Masquerading with Dr. Charming

## HEALTH CARE HEROES BOOK 7

JESSICA PARKER

SILVER SPINDLE PRODUCTIONS LLC

*For my family that works in the medical field. Thank you for tirelessly and selflessly serving those in need of your skills.*

# Chapter One

Sofie and I ran through the park, the fall morning air held just a snap of cold from the rain the night before. The red and yellow leaves had reached their full autumn glory, making it look as if the trees were on fire.

A perfect day for a run through Crestfield Park, especially for my long run. I'd definitely earned all the donuts from the bakery on Main Street after running two miles. The thought of it had me drooling like one of Pavlov's dogs. Forget the bell, just picturing the freshly glazed apple fritter made me want to run home before reaching my three mile mark. I really wished I had time to get one this morning.

But I wasn't running for myself, the race in three weeks was raising funds for cancer research. It was like a sign from the universe as the race date coincided with the anniversary of when mom passed from breast cancer.

"You okay?" Sofie asked.

"Thinking about my mom."

Sofie was the best running partner I had, and I'd miss

her when she moved to the big city. But she had plans for her life that didn't include sticking around the small town run by the rich upper class.

Sofie's smile faded. "Ten years?"

I nodded. I didn't really like to talk about Mom being gone. The advantage of having a best friend, meant she knew the details and I didn't have to say it out loud. Sofie let the subject drop as we continued our morning run.

We made it around the curve of the trail without another soul in sight. A fact I was grateful for when I slipped on a wet leaf a minute later. My arms flapped out like a baby bird, as I clumsily got my feet under me.

As soon as I was sure I wouldn't fall, I looked at Sofie, her eyes wide with amusement, and a laugh burst out from her.

"Is that a new running move?" she asked between giggles.

I laughed with her. "The bird flap is all the rage in the European race circuit."

We laughed more, and any remaining somberness about my mother's passing dissipated as we returned to our running rhythm.

"Excited to be back in your house?" Sofie asked.

I groaned. "It'll be another two weeks at least."

"Wasn't it supposed to be done last Friday?"

I nodded. "My flooring was delayed. Apparently the supplier oversold their inventory. They offered an upgrade as compensation, but it won't get here for a couple more weeks. With Courtney's wedding coming up, I don't know when I can be there to let them in for installation."

Sofie chuckled. "How are the wedding festivities coming along?"

I grimaced and brushed a sweaty dark strand of hair off my forehead, it had come loose from my ponytail at some point and I'd been battling it for the last lap. "If I have to hear Courtney talk about setting me up with her fiancé's cousin one more time I'm going to tell her I have a work emergency."

Sofie arched an eyebrow. "What kind of convention planning emergency would require you to miss a wedding?"

I shrugged. "The hard part would be hiding while I live with Dad and the step-monster."

"You can crash on my couch."

I laughed, "Your couch has more lumps than day-old oatmeal."

She playfully pushed my shoulder. "It's not that bad."

"It's the reason I moved out."

We hadn't lived together for a year now. I knew the day the for sale sign went up on the little cottage house that it was meant for me. What I hadn't known is that the old pipes would cause the main floor of my house to flood while I was out of town running a comic convention. I was lucky that the insurance covered most of the damage. I just wished that the contractor they approved would take care of things faster.

She rolled her eyes. "Want to get a bear claw for breakfast?"

"Can't, Step-monster scheduled the final dress fittings for this morning. I'm on a strict grapefruit diet for breakfast this morning."

We finished our morning run, and Sofie headed north

towards Main Street while I turned west to loop back to Sycamore Way for my dad's neighborhood.

He'd sold my childhood home and retired in a gated villa on the hill of Crestfield. The back of the house overlooked the park, while the front of the house wasn't quite in position to see the ocean. Stepmom had complained many times about the lack of ocean view. If they'd bought the house two doors up, then they'd have been able to see the beach.

Dad, however, was happy to have saved the money and walk up the street for the view when he wanted to look at it.

Why he'd ever picked her, I had no clue.

Victoria did not do anything common, and she certainly did not settle for less than satisfaction. Instead she plotted and maneuvered for what she wanted until she got it. About six months after moving into their new house, Dad had a rooftop garden built so she could sit up there and see the ocean when she desired.

I ran closer to the park exit I needed, slowing to pass a man stretching by a bench. He nodded and smiled as I passed.

Just another runner enjoying the cool autumn air. Except he wasn't just a random runner. I had to do a double take, as the first glance made me wonder if my eyes were deceiving me.

He had to be one of the most handsome men I'd ever seen. Crestfield had a lot of good looking men. After all, Crestfield was home to many of the rich, and rumored to be famous.

I snuck a look over my shoulder at him.

He was tall and lean, with well groomed light brown

hair and a short beard. His build showed he wasn't skimping at the gym either. A smile spread across his lips, and he lifted a hand to wave at me.

An embarrassed flush burned on my cheeks at being caught staring.

I whipped my head around, and saw a flash of yellow on the path. The heel of my right foot landed on the pile of wet leaves. Momentum kept me moving, my weight shifting forward. The leaves slipped, and I might as well have been in a cartoon.

Surely none of the animated banana peels could compare to the slick leaves. All the arm flapping, and feet fumbling, in the world couldn't save me as I went flying forward.

The ground rose, my arms instinctively rising to brace my fall. My hands scraped across the rough pathway.

Stunned, out of breath, I laid there as I assessed what hurt more, my hands or my pride.

I rolled over onto my back before sitting up. In the process of moving, pain flared in my ankle. I let out a pained groan.

The man from by the bench rushed to my side.

"Where does it hurt?"

I pointed at my right foot.

"Can I take a look at it?"

I nodded.

He shifted to look at it more closely. Then gently began examining my foot much like a doctor. Asking if I could move it, or if it hurt when he touched on either side of the ankle bone.

He cleared his throat. "Looks like a sprain, although an x-ray would rule out any fractures."

"Are you a doctor or something?" I asked when he'd finished.

A corner of his lips turned up in a smile. "Where are my manners? Dr. Bradley Charmaine."

"Bethany Spencer. Friends call me Beth."

"Well Beth it's not every day I have a beautiful woman fall for me."

My jaw dropped as I let loose a surprised laugh. "You did not just use a line like that."

He winked and I flushed once more as I looked into his gorgeous hazel eyes.

"I'm sorry that you're hurt, but I'm not sorry that it gave me the opportunity to talk to you."

"Say that to all your patients?"

"Hardly. Think you can stand, Beth?" He rose and extended a hand to help me up.

I lifted my hand, and saw all the scrapes from the pavement across my palms.

"Quite the road rash you've got there," he said as he looked at the tender skin.

"Any recommendations Doctor?"

"Soap and water to start." He bypassed my hands in favor of gripping my uninjured forearms to help me to my feet. But as soon as I put weight on my right ankle the pain roared to life.

I hissed at the pain, and lifted my injured foot.

"Here." He looped one arm behind me, before bending to sweep me up into his arms.

I felt very much like a heroine in a movie being rescued.

Although I hardly needed rescuing from my own clumsiness.

"Did you drive here?" he set me on the bench where I'd first seen him.

"Don't you think that defeats the purpose of running?" I asked.

"Not if it allows me to get an apple fritter after my morning run. If I had to run to the bakery from here, they'd be out before I reached main street."

If he wasn't such a flirt, and I hadn't sworn off relationships, I could have fallen for him right then and there.

"Tell me Doctor—"

"Brad, you haven't filled out enough paperwork to be a patient."

I smiled. "Brad then, any chance you could help me convince my stepmom that a Danish pastry is a perfectly suitable breakfast? She's convinced that anything more than half a grapefruit is garish."

He chuckled. "Sounds like she'd get along fine with my mother. I'm still trying to convince her that pie is a perfectly suitable serving of fruit."

I laughed. "But is your mother pestering you to lose a few inches so you can get a date to a wedding?"

"No. She's just trying to auction me off."

Playing along I gave a dramatic gasp worthy of any stage. "She isn't!" I declared.

"She most certainly is. You are in the presence of one of the most eligible bachelors of the Harvest Ball Festival."

"Your life must be so difficult. Women throwing money at you for a good cause." I rolled my eyes. "Maybe you should find someone you like to bid on you."

"Are you volunteering?"

"Only if you'll agree to be my date to my stepsister's wedding," I half joked.

Courtney would probably have an aneurysm if I added another guest to her list this close to the wedding. I'd been allotted a plus one, but I knew she thought I'd show up alone. I'd overheard my stepmother talking to the wedding planner about removing the extra place setting.

When a beat passed and he hadn't responded to my joke, I decided to move the conversation along.

"Don't you need to be saving someone's life soon?"

He checked the time on his fancy smartwatch. The watch was far too shiny to have been made with any plastic bits like my own scuffed lime green watch.

He looked back at me. "I won't abandon you here, so back to my earlier question. How can I help you get home safely?"

"I live in the neighborhood over there." I pointed towards the entrance of the park and the houses visible through the trees.

"Perfect, my car is parked near the entrance. Please let me assist you home."

"That's very gentlemanly of you, but I as an embarrassed, *not distressed*, damsel, can get home on my own."

"Rush hour traffic is starting up, I can't leave you to hobble home on an injured ankle. You could get hurt even more. As a gentleman and a doctor I couldn't possibly abandon you."

# Chapter Two

He lifted me into his arms once more and pretty soon we were by his car. Although, *car* was too modest a name for the sleek machinery before me. The dark teal colored space car looked like it belonged in a movie with super spies. He set me down on my good foot while he opened the passenger door for me. The seat was low to the floor, which was saying something considering how low to the ground the car was.

"Are you sure that's a car?" I asked, as he put his arm around me to help me balance. "I'm pretty sure I saw it in a movie with robots."

"Yep. It's a Lamborghini." He tensed as if bracing for my reaction.

I let out a soft whistle before joking, "Please tell me you're not a secret agent."

He laughed, and I could feel it vibrating in his chest due to our close proximity.

"You've found me out," he said, even as he let out one more chuckle.

I looked up into his eyes, as he gazed down at me. The world started to fade away, and heat rose in my cheeks the longer we stared at each other.

"Dr. Brad! Is that you?" A woman squealed.

The moment broke, awareness of our surroundings rushed in. Cars sped by as morning traffic was in full swing. My blush heated into a full flush of embarrassment as I realized people I knew were staring in our direction. The woman yelling at Brad, was across the street leaning out of the window of a hot pink jeep that probably belonged in a reality TV series with rich wives.

He waved politely at the woman across the street. "Hi Mrs. Willison."

The way she looked at Brad, like he was a tasty snack, didn't seem appropriate for a married woman.

"I look forward to seeing you later today."

"I didn't realize little Jimmy had an appointment at the office. I'll make sure to save him a superhero sticker."

The car behind Mrs. Willison honked. She looked flustered for only a moment before flashing him a .... smile. "I look forward to bidding on you at the Harvest Ball." She sped off before Brad could respond.

Brad helped me as I worked my way to sitting inside the car. The soft leather seat felt like sitting on a cloud, the car was so smooth it didn't even jostle my tender ankle.

"Aside from my boss's car, this has to be the best thing I've ever ridden in." I relaxed further into the seat now that the seat warmer had heated up the leather seats.

The drive to my house was short, but it felt longer due to the inordinate amount of people staring at us as we passed. At a stop sign, one of the neighborhood gossips, a woman in a magenta velvet tracksuit, took photos of his car. She didn't even bother trying to hide her efforts as she pointed her bedazzled phone our way.

"That's going to be all over social media," I said.

He shrugged.

"It doesn't bother you that people will start rumors that we're in a relationship or something?" I gestured at his car. "Clearly we're in different leagues. I prefer a car that I'm not worried about eating seven layers of nachos in."

"Truth be told I much prefer that too."

I pointed to my dad's house with a light blue door. "It's that one."

Minutes later he had his arm around my waist, while I had one around his shoulder for support, as I hobbled towards the door. I refused to be carried again, as I didn't want a picture of that ending up online.

The door to the house swung open and my stepsister stood scowling in the doorway. She was wearing a knee-length cream dress, with a sash over the top that stated *Bride* in pink sparkly letters. Her auburn hair was half up with lots of ringlets twisted up into some style she'd probably picked out of a fancy french magazine at the salon. Apparently that was a thing, women voluntarily scheduled hours of their day to have someone poke them with hair pins and cement their hair with enough hairspray to glaze a ham.

Brad didn't say anything, but I felt him straighten next to me as she looked first at the car, then him. Clearly she was doing calculations on how much he was worth. Then she looked at me as if she was wondering why someone like him would be with someone like me. Clearly she didn't think I was worthy of someone who could afford a car like the one he drove.

A glance at his face showed that his friendly demeanor had changed into one more guarded.

"Brad, this is Courtney. Courtney this is —"

Brad finished for me. "I'm her boyfriend."

My jaw dropped open and I stared at him in surprise.

"Is he your plus one?" Courtney asked, still looking at him. "I need to know now. The wedding planner wanted finalized seating arrangements yesterday, but I can probably change it if I know now."

"Yes, I am." Brad said before I could answer. "It took me a while to reschedule my patient appointments at the clinic."

This could not be happening. Sure I'd joked earlier with him that I should find a pretend date. But I would have made it clear if I thought he'd take it seriously.

Courtney looked at his car. "Are you a doctor or something?"

"Something," he answered.

"Easton is going to be disappointed, he was looking forward to seeing you again Beth," she turned to Brad. "He's my fiancé's cousin, we've been trying to set her up with him ever since the engagement party."

I cringed. "Seeing him once was enough."

Brad coughed to cover a laugh.

Courtney clucked her tongue. "We need to leave in fifteen minutes or we'll be late for the dress fitting."

She turned and walked into the house, presumably to get her mother. Brad started to step forward, but I gripped his arm to stop him.

I lowered my voice so it wouldn't carry inside the house, "What was that?"

"I'm sorry, the way she looked at you like you weren't worthy, I hate to see people treated like that. Your suggestion earlier popped into my mind, and the boyfriend thing tumbled out."

"You mean my joke from earlier? I barely know you."

"I know. But maybe we can help each other out. I'll be your date for her wedding and keep the creepy cousin away. You can win me at the auction and I don't end up with someone like Mrs. Willison winning."

I cringed, my resistance cracking. I really didn't want to spend the reception hiding from the creepy cousin.

"I've watched enough movies to know this arrangement doesn't turn out well. You just told Courtney you're my boyfriend and she's probably inside telling the rest of my family right now."

"The attention will be on Courtney at the wedding. I'll smile for pictures and bore people with stories about foot fungus or something at dinner so they don't ask too many questions. We can fake it for a few hours. The ball won't require more than a dance and a photo or two."

"I need to know more than your approval of Bear Claws and taste in cars to fake a relationship."

He pounced on my fading resistance. "I'll happily take you out on as many dates as it takes."

"Real *fake* dates?"

I shifted back to get a better look at his face, and the pain flared hot and bright once more in my ankle. The pain had started to dull, but the flare had me hissing like a wet cat. My face scrunched up of its own accord and I closed my eyes so I didn't have to look at Brad's handsome face.

This was just one reason of many for why I would be single the rest of my life, I couldn't be a graceful damsel in distress. Courtney would have swooned like a Hollywood socialite. My stepmother would have been more grand, like a high lady in a Regency romance novel gracefully simpering and garnishing sympathy.

"Let's get your foot wrapped, propped up, and put ice on it." Brad picked me up into his arms. "We can work out the details when you come to my office later for me to take an x-ray."

"You don't need to carry me." I protested weakly.

I still hadn't opened my eyes, and maybe that was why the smell of him caught my attention. He should be all sweaty and gross from running, like gym socks. But no, he had to smell like fancy car leather, and smoked spices.

"What kind of boyfriend do you think I am?"

I laughed and opened my eyes. We were inside the house and entering the living room. I pointed him to a baby blue wingback chair by the white brick fireplace.

"Beth, are you alright?" My dad asked as he entered from the doorway that led to his study.

"I sprained my ankle."

Brad set me down in the chair, and then turned to shake my dad's hand. Introductions were made, and I tried to keep my face less surprised as I observed the shocked expressions of both my father and stepmother at the word boyfriend.

Victoria regained her senses first and smoothed her

expression into a polite smile. "Courtney told me, but I didn't believe it."

Brad looked at them sweetly. "It's my fault. I wanted to keep Beth all to myself for a bit longer."

Dad smiled, "She told us that she had a plus one for the wedding, but I just thought she meant Sofie."

I wanted to smack myself. Sofie would have been the best plus one for Courtney's wedding. She knew of my family drama, and I'd have someone to help keep an eye out for Easton.

"Mom." Courtney stomped into the room with her purse on her shoulder. "The dress fitting."

Victoria looked at the dainty silver watch on her wrist. "Of course, we must be going."

Dad looked at me, then Victoria. "She can't walk. Can you reschedule?"

"No!" Courtney screeched. She started hyperventilating with short fast breaths that made her sound like a panting miniature poodle.

Brad looked at her in alarm.

Victoria patted Courtney's back soothingly, "It's been scheduled for months."

Dad and Victoria continued to discuss options for the dress fitting.

Brad looked down at me. "Any chance you have a bandage or brace I could use for you?"

"It's under the sink in the bathroom." I pointed towards the hall "Second door on the left."

When Brad stepped out of the room I whistled to get my family's attention. "Courtney, I can make the adjustments myself. I'm going to be staying off my foot so it'll be better by your wedding and I'll need something to do aside from watching TV."

"Can she do that?" Courtney asked her mother.

Dad nodded. "She's been making her Halloween costumes for years. Her mother taught her how."

"I thought you bought those," Courtney said. "You made that princess dress you wore last year at the festival?"

"Yep." I popped the *p* on the word.

Courtney relaxed, and she stopped hyperventilating. "Your dress won't look horrible?"

I shook my head.

My Stepmother's jaw dropped. "I thought you were just being rude when you told me the fabric store on main street was where you bought it."

I shrugged. "Technically I did buy most of it there. The rest of it was stuff I already had."

I'd never tried to keep it a secret that I made my costumes, I worked for a comic convention planning company after all. But I had stopped talking about it since no one in my family understood my passion for cosplay. I couldn't wait for the flooring in my house to be done so that I could fill the guest room with the feathers, wings, and fabrics for my various cosplay ideas. The apartment I'd shared with Sofie wasn't big enough for it, and I no longer had an office to store things in since my boss decided we could do things virtually. Considering he travelled three weeks of the month, it was a miracle we'd had an office to begin with.

My dad fussed over Courtney and my stepmother before seeing them out to Victoria's car. The room was empty when Brad returned. He carefully wrapped my foot, and it gave me time to study him. I could do worse in the fake dating department. Judging by his car he was a successful, handsome doctor that was kind enough to help a stranger in the park.

"Ice it and elevate it, until you can get to my office." He instructed. He pulled out his phone from his running shorts, and swiped across the screen. "I have an opening at two."

"I don't even know where your office is."

"I'll text you the address."

We exchanged numbers, and I felt my phone chirp in my own pocket when he sent me his information. He gave me some more instructions on taking care of my ankle.

An alarm sounded on his phone. "I have to get to work."

"I'd see you to the door, but a doctor told me to stay off my foot."

He grinned and a dimple popped on his cheek. My stomach flip flopped in a good way.

"I'll see you at two."

After I saw him take off in his ridiculously fancy car through the window, I waited for my dad to come back. He'd no doubt have questions about my new boyfriend I didn't want to answer.

With my foot on the ottoman, I wasn't surprised when my dad brought me an ice pack from the freezer.

"Want to tell me how my daughter, who has proclaimed she'll be single forever, has a boyfriend?" he asked.

I shrugged. "I needed a date for Courtney's wedding."

"And you found a boyfriend in the process?"

"It's not like I'll marry him," I said.

All my relationships were temporary. I'd seen what my dad went through when my mom died. I'd lived what it had been like to lose my mom as a child. Her and my dad were my whole world, and her death devastated me in a way that words couldn't do justice. I didn't ever want to live through that again, so I was never going to have someone close enough for me to lose.

My dad patted my arm. "Give it a chance, Beth. You might be surprised."

My dad left me on the chair and went back to his study. I pulled out my phone and decided to catch up on the latest cosplay making videos. I needed to be prepared for the convention my boss was thinking about next spring.

Hours later I'd hobbled into the kitchen and scarfed down a bowl of sugary cereal from the box I'd smuggled into the pantry behind the bag of actual sugar when I'd moved home. I'd then made myself comfortable at the breakfast table with my foot propped on a chair. The kitchen was the best place to get fresh ice.

Courtney and Victoria came in with a takeout box that smelled like fish.

"We brought you left overs," Courtney said, setting the takeout box on the table in front of me. "It'll probably need to be reheated. It got cold in the trunk while we were shopping."

I peaked in the box, hoping she wasn't saying what I thought she'd said. But of course, I'd understood what she'd said correctly. Inside the cardboard box was a half-eaten salmon fillet. Courtney or Victoria had obviously eaten the other half. I'd pass on eating it for that alone. But the second reason I decided to pass was my appointment with

Brad at his office. I'd have to reheat the fish in the microwave to leave on time.

Microwaved fish was the worst, it would transform even the most delicious fish into something fit for a dumpster. Hard pass. Victoria entered the kitchen carrying a zipped up garment bag.

"Thanks, but I have to be going," I said.

Victoria looked at me sharply. "Where are you off to?"

"Doctor appointment for my ankle."

"You can't drive on it."

I showed her my phone where the rideshare app was displayed. The driver was nearing my house.

"I got it covered." I put my phone in my pocket, and slowly worked my way outside.

# Chapter Three

A snail on a tortoise moved faster than me, hobbling into the waiting room at Brad's clinic. The small clinic was attached to the main hospital in town. The receptionist gave me a curious glance as she took my name down, told me to take a seat, and didn't ask for me to fill out any insurance paperwork. I hoped I wouldn't get billed for this later. I wasn't dirt poor, but I wasn't rich either. A medical bill could be the difference between replacing my water logged couch or sitting on my new floor.

The coffee table held the traditional gossip and home décor magazines. I briefly rifled through them before finding one that peaked my interest. The heading suggested an inside look at the recently announced superhero movie *Ice Princess*.

I picked it up just as a nurse called my name.

Figuring I'd have to wait more in an exam room, I took the magazine with me. Instead of taking me straight to an exam room after checking my blood pressure as well as height and weight, she wheeled me to a room in the main hospital for x-rays.

Once those were done, I was finally guided back to a typical exam room with the crinkly paper on the exam table.

I opted for the little chair instead while I read the magazine. The inside look at the movie didn't offer much. Just rehashed the taglines for the comic, and speculated if Sasha Smith would be able to meet fan expectations. She definitely looked the part in her costume, but I hadn't seen her in anything to speculate on her talent.

"I hope the writers come up with a good story and the director doesn't make it all about explosions."

I looked up to find Brad in the doorway. He was dressed in slacks and a button up white shirt, the traditional doctor coat over top with a blue stethoscope around his neck.

"Comic fan?" I asked hopefully.

"One of my best friends is really into them. He introduced me to the best ones."

"He has excellent taste if he introduced you to the *Ice Princess*."

Brad smiled. "I found that one on my own."

My stomach fluttered and I looked away to set the magazine down along with my purse.

"How do I pay for this appointment, Doctor Brad?"

He waved his hand away. "I can't date my patients, and I can't charge my girlfriend."

"That leaves us in a quandary then, because the nice nurse did x-rays, and I'm on your office schedule."

He shifted uncomfortably, "I've got the x-rays covered, and this is my lunch break."

I gasped. "You are not working on your lunch! Work breaks are sacred."

"I'll eat while I do paperwork."

"Don't you have more appointments?"

"My last afternoon appointment was rescheduled this morning."

"How do you not have a real girlfriend?" I asked. "You're handsome, kind, courteous, and love comics?"

"My career is too demanding for the white picket fence plan. I saw a lot of people divorcing in medical school, and now all I find in the dating pool are people that want the prestige of marrying a doctor. They all want to be seen with me, not stay home and play board games or watch a movie."

My heart went out to him. But I understood what he was saying. Marriage and relationships weren't right for some people. It was the same thing I'd tried to explain to my Dad about myself for many years. I'd had a couple boyfriends in college, but I didn't want to put anyone through the pain of losing me if I got the same cancer my mom had.

"So gold diggers?"

"You have no idea."

"As your fake girlfriend, I will do my best to fight them off of you."

"I appreciate that. What about you? Any men I need to duel?"

"No. I date here and there. Easton's related to the groom and can't take a hint."

"And he's the reason you don't do relationships?"

I shook my head. "I don't really know you, so this is a lot to dump on you, but if we're really doing this my dad could bring it up. I haven't wanted a relationship since I found out I carry the gene for the same cancer my mom had."

"I'm sorry about your mother."

My fingers fidgeted with a lock of my dark hair, and I decided to change the subject before he could ask more questions.

"How does this fake relationship work? What are the rules?" I asked.

"Well, I need you to win me at the ball to avoid the gold diggers."

"I'm in the middle of house renovations, how much do you think it will be?"

"I'll get you a card to pay with."

"Thank you. I just need a date for my stepsister's wedding. Do you have a tux? I can get you one if you don't."

"I have a tux set aside just for secret missions like this." He winked.

Laughter burst out of me, and pulled out my phone to give him the dates for the wedding rehearsal and wedding.

He looked at his calendar, "I can make both days work."

We paused, and I fidgeted with the strap on my watch.

"So what do the x-rays say?" I asked.

He opened a screen on his tablet to show me. "Nothing broken, just a sprain like I thought. Is it feeling any better after resting it this morning?"

I nodded. "Yes, still hobbling, but the ice, wrap you did earlier, and a couple pain pills have helped a lot."

"Try to baby it for a few more days. I can give you

crutches for the times you need to move around if you'd like."

I shook my head. "If I don't need them, I'd rather not."

We chatted for a bit about my options before settling on a brace. It would be faster and easier than trying to wrap it with a long bandage every day. And I'd be less likely to accidently cut off circulation to my toes.

There was a tap on the door, and Brad looked at his watch.

He looked at me apologetically. "My lunch break is almost over."

My time with him was dwindling, but I didn't feel like I knew him well enough to pull off the charade. I'd need fake dates, or people would be able to tell we were strangers. We'd only gotten away with it this morning because of the dress fitting stress and my injury.

"We should get a donut or something." He looked confused, so I kept going to explain myself. "The fake dates. We need to get to know each other more. I'd meet you for a run in the park, but it looks like it will be a bit before I can do that."

He smiled, and it calmed the nerves in my belly.

"Would Friday night at the fall festival work for you? Your foot should be doing much better by then, and we can grab an apple cider donut and chili for dinner."

Now it was my turn to smile. "That sounds perfect. Would you mind if we stop by my company's booth while we're there?"

"Not a problem. I'll pick you up at five?"

I nodded, and the door to the room opened. The nurse poked her head in, her brown hair tied up in a bun.

"Excuse me, Doctor Charmaine, there's a worried patient hoping to speak with you on line one."

I called another car to take me home. I needed to rest my foot so that it would be ready for my donut date with Brad. My fake donut date. Although it sounded like a real date, I'd have to pay for my own food to keep it securely in the fake date realm. But he was picking me up, which was more of an effort than my last real date had made. My last date had made me drive since his car was impounded, and he'd spent the entire time complaining about how I drove.

Brad didn't seem like the kind of person who would do that. Meeting him was the highlight of my Monday.

# Chapter Four

Friday afternoon I spent fixing the snowflake lace on the ice fairy gloves for the booth at fall fest. I was donating several of my old cosplays for the booth, and needed to drop off the gloves tonight.

My phone rang and I grinned when I saw that it was Sofie calling.

"How is the book beast treating you?" I asked.

She groaned. "I hate whoever they are."

For the last few months someone had trolled Sofie's book recommendations with snarky comments against her favorite books on the library website. Sofie had started a book blog on the library's website to try and get more interest from the public. So far the only interest people had was in the comments of user1775. The local paper had written a short piece wondering about who the commenter could be, and thus the name Book Beast was born.

"What did they do now?" I asked.

"They said that Jane Austen's works are painful to read and an affront to the English language."

I cringed. If there was one author that Sofie loved above all others, it was Austen.

"Did you respond?"

"Of course I responded. I had to set the public straight. The book club ladies brought me cookies to celebrate my great retort to the troll's comments."

The local ladies met once a week in one of the library rooms and had been sneaking cookies in for the last twenty years. The librarians had let the no food policy slide so long as they got served the legendary snickerdoodles.

"Do we need to watch the six hour Pride and Prejudice movie?" I asked.

She laughed. "No, it's alright. I won't make you sit on my terrible couch."

"I would for you."

"Thanks. Are we running tomorrow morning?"

I'd texted her earlier that my foot was feeling better today.

"I'll ask Brad tonight if I'm clear to run."

"Ask him if he understands the merits of Austen."

I snorted. "Leave him out of it. We're helping each other through awkward social situations."

He'd texted me throughout the last few days, and even called a couple times. I now knew his favorite and least favorite superhero, and he knew I hadn't yet streamed the latest season of the Fire Storm superhero series. We both had strong objections to spoiling movies for other people and he'd invited me to watch the series with him once the craziness of the fall festival ball was over.

"I still can't believe you're going to be his fake girlfriend to get him out of the bachelor auction. What money are you supposed to use to buy him? The website has comments with people saying they'll bid thousands on him."

"You can't be serious."

"How can you not be watching it? The highest bidder is adamant that they'd spend five grand to win him?"

"You really need to stop reading the comments."

"You've got some competition is all I'm trying to say. People are still talking about the picture of you and him from Monday."

I groaned. I'd had to hear all week how distasteful Courtney and Victoria thought the photo was. The camera angle had not been flattering, but Brad had definitely looked good. Why was it that I could dress up in my best clothes and run errands around town only to not see one person I knew. But if I decided to wear my ugliest comfortable sweatpants and a messy bun, I'd run into every high school mean girl that still remembered me, and somehow end up in the background of a viral photo for my town.

"Are we still on for movie night tomorrow?" I asked to change the subject.

I could hear her smile through the phone as she said, "I've got barbeque chicken pizza scheduled to be delivered."

We chatted through our movie options, although we both knew we'd be watching our all time favorite Halloween movie, *Hocus Pocus*. There was just something wonderful about quoting the lines back and forth and wondering how we ever thought the little sister running from the witch wasn't annoying.

We chatted a little longer before hanging up so I could clean up before Brad got to my house. As I put away my scissors, needle and thread, I saw the garment bag from the bridal shop. I still needed to try it on and make any final adjustments. They'd be minor, but it would be best to make them soon so I had plenty of time to do it properly.

Time passed quickly as I put the bag of things to take to the fair together. Safety pins, glitter, various colors of duct tape, and a travel sewing kit in addition to the costume accessories went into the duffle bag. I had my small purse with lip gloss, wallet, and phone also ready for when Brad arrived.

My ankle was feeling a lot better, I didn't need any pain pills, and could move around the house without hobbling around the furniture. I still wore the brace, but the swelling was pretty much gone. There was a little bruising that I hoped would go away since it was still a bit tender.

At five, Brad's car parked in front of my house. He wasn't driving the teal robot car this time. Instead he drove a black SUV, it looked too shiny to have been used often for any dirt roads. When we were both in the car I waited for him to pull onto the road, before asking.

"Am I in witness protection now?" I asked.

"I thought it was better than a robot car."

"Where is the robot car? Is it fighting other robot cars?"

"I returned it. A friend let me borrow it while this was getting repaired."

"Your friend just let you drive the space car?"

Brad shrugged. "He is out of town a lot, and it's not good for the cars to sit for long periods of time."

I let out a low whistle. "Your friend is a nice person. So is this your normal car?"

He nodded. "I don't need much in a car. Just something that is reliable and gets me around town."

We spent the rest of the drive scanning through different radio stations and deciding on the worst and best music genres. Rock was superior to country, but country beat out rap. It didn't take long to arrive at the park near the pier where the booths for the festival were. Carnival rides were set up on the far end of the park, while the vendor booths were lined in rows. The smell of cinnamon, apples, and pumpkins filled my nose, while the sound of laughter and excited chatter filled the air.

I lifted my purse onto my shoulder, and when I reached for my duffle, Brad took it for me.

"You don't have to carry that," I said.

"I know, but as your boyfriend, I'd like to."

"Thanks."

He paid for our tickets to the festival entrance fee, and we decided to drop off the duffel before going in search of food. Brad so far didn't seem to have any flaws. He was the perfect date, not that we were dating. I certainly wasn't interested in dating.

"What do you do for work?" Brad asked me.

"I help coordinate conventions across the country." It was my standard answer.

Enough detail that people who weren't interested would stop asking, and not enough for me to embarrass myself by exposing my love of cosplay, and nerd culture.

"What type?" He asked. "My friend Scott plans comic conventions. I don't think he'll ever grow up."

"Comic Conventions are no joke. They take a lot of care to please the fan base."

"Sure, but don't you think it's sad that adults dress up and play pretend?"

With those few words, I'd found the first flaw in Brad. I was grateful I hadn't told him more about what I did. Although the booth would give it away. I quickly decided to stick to my generic answers about coordinating vendors, staff, and speakers for the events. He didn't need to know that I loved the events centered around pop culture, comics, and other fan favorites.

"Well," I pointed at the booth I needed to drop the bag off at. "Cosplay can do a lot."

*Cosplay for a Cause. Cancer Run, October 29th* was written across the banner.

He grimaced. "I'm sorry, I didn't mean that the way that sounded."

"You did. But I'd like you to meet Marie. She's the brilliant mind behind this booth."

Marie was old enough to be my grandmother, and she'd been one of my biggest supporters when it came to cosplay.

"Beth!" Marie happily called out to me from behind her table.

"How are the sign ups?" I asked.

"Slow, but the first day usually is. Who's this handsome fellow?"

I quickly make introductions. "Brad, Marie's foundation raises money for cancer research, and to help families with loved ones that are dealing with cancer."

Brad shook her hand while saying, "It's a pleasure to meet you. How can I help?"

Marie told him her story. She'd lost her husband to cancer, and then years later she lost her son to the same disease. She'd started raising money for research in hope that no one else would have to lose their loved ones. Comics had been the escape her men had needed during their treatments. Her story was sad, real, and I hadn't met anyone that wasn't affected by hearing it. By the time she gave him her pitch on the run and charity, Brad had his card out. I was happy to watch as he signed up for the run, and made a donation.

Her story typically garnered this response. It was part of why she was the face of the charity. Marie moved people, and caused people to feel. I'd felt that loss with my mom, I understood a fraction of the loss Marie had faced. I wouldn't do that to anyone. I wouldn't leave a husband or child behind when I died someday from cancer.

As we walked away from the booth I told him thank you.

"For what?"

"Really listening to her. You considered her words."

He shrugged. "Maybe I just wanted to impress the girl."

"You have."

He took my hand in his. "Well, let me get you the best donut you've ever tasted just to make sure."

"Deal."

He didn't let go of my hand, and I found myself liking the comfortable way we walked together in search of pastries and chili.

We found the chili first, and while it was good, I preferred my dad's homemade recipe. By the time we got to the booth advertising apple cider donuts the smell of cider was making my mouth water. Brad had refused to let me pay for the chili, and it was no different with the donut.

He handed me the warm desert. It looked like a cross between a glazed cake donut, and a crumb donut. But the taste had to be the best thing I'd ever had. Cinnamon, nutmeg, and sugar exploded on my tongue as I bit into the cake donut. It tasted like everything good about fall.

"So good," I said between bites.

"I'm so glad you're enjoying yourself." An older woman said as she approached.

# Chapter Five

She wore a chocolate colored business suit, it looked like it had been pressed, and was spotless. It made her stand out from the crowd, and I felt underdressed in my jeans and ivory colored sweater. I quickly used a napkin and tried to remove the sticky sugar from my hand if she wanted to shake in greeting.

The woman stopped next to Brad and turned to him. "Bradley, I didn't know you would be here."

"Mother." Brad gave the woman a quick kiss on her cheek, careful to not get sugar from his donut on his mother's clothes.

When they stepped apart, she glanced at me like I was a piece of gum stuck to the bottom of her Louboutin heel. "Who's this?"

Brad slid an arm around my shoulders and pulled me to his side. "This is my girlfriend, Beth."

"When did this happen?" she asked, her tone cold.

I could feel him tensing beside me, we hadn't quite figured out all the details of our fake dating history.

"Recently," I said.

"We didn't want the country club gossips finding out, while we were getting to know each other," he added.

She frowned. "So you let an old woman with a penchant for succulents announce it with that tacky photo. It looked like it was taken with a phone's camera."

"I sprained my ankle, he was helping me home. It couldn't be avoided."

Her tone was cold as she said, "It can always be avoided."

I had to bite my tongue so I wouldn't say something that would make things more difficult for Brad. She was still his mother, even if she was an incredibly rude woman.

"Excuse us, Mother. We were done enjoying all the festival has to offer." Brad turned us to walk away.

"Bradley Charmaine. We need to discuss your role as one of the Bachelors at the Masquerade Ball."

"If it wasn't for Jack, I wouldn't be involved. He can give me any details I need."

"Your costume is at the tailors, you need to get it fitted."

"Have a good evening, Mother."

We left her standing there, and while I was happy to be away, I worried for Brad.

"I don't think she cares if you have a girlfriend or not."

He snorted. "She only cares if I live up to her expectations, and keep up appearances."

"Does she always arrange your clothing?"

"It's easier to let her pick what she wants me to wear to events than fight with her. I wore a regular silk tie instead of a bow tie with my tux once, and she still talks about how it ruined the photos."

His disdain for cosplay was starting to make sense. "I can see why you don't like costumes."

He looked at me with a lifted brow.

"You've had to pretend to be someone you're not for her too many times. Wearing the costumes for the role she demanded you play. Cosplay isn't about dressing up to please other people. It's about dressing up in something that inspires you, and brings you joy."

"You make it sound like fun."

"Well you'll get a chance to try it."

"What do you mean?"

"The race you signed up for, it's in costume."

His shoulders tensed up tighter than when he first saw his mother. "I thought costumes were optional?"

"They are, but it's more fun to run in costume."

"Have you already picked out what you'll dress up as?"

"A tortoise naturally."

"Naturally?"

"Because the tortoise wins the race."

His laugh shook away the last of the tension in his shoulders.

"Want to look at the rest of the booths, or take a whirl on the ferris wheel?"

"I think I spotted a booth with darts earlier. I'd like to try my luck at winning a giant fuzzy stuffed animal."

"Not if I win it first."

We made our way through the rows to the balloon dart game. The wall in the booth was covered with red, yellow, and white balloons. Brad refused to let me pay once again, and we were each given three darts while the attendant went over the rules. The red balloons were worth a small plastic sword, the yellow balloons were worth a plastic tiara, the white balloon was worth a stuffed animal. They had a plush frog prince, a flower shaped throw pillow, and a giant stuffed unicorn. To get the big unicorn it required hitting the white balloon with all three darts.

I picked up the first dart and Brad picked up one as well.

"Ladies first." He waved a hand at the balloons.

I took a deep breath, weighed the dart in my hand, and picked the white balloon I wanted to hit. I threw it and the white balloon gave a satisfying pop when I hit my target.

Brad gave a cheer, and then it was his turn to throw. He also hit a white balloon.

The booth attendant clapped, and placed two five-inch plush teddy bears on the counter.

"I'm going for the unicorn." I said as I picked up my second dart.

I hit my second white balloon, leaving two white balloons on the wall. There wasn't enough for us both to win a unicorn.

Brad took his turn, and also hit a white balloon.

He turned to me. "There's one white balloon left. Throw at the same time?"

I nodded, and we stepped close to each other. "On three."

A breeze blew through the carnival rows, and the balloon wiggled in an attempt to escape the tape holding it to the board. We counted down, and threw our third dart together. My dart hit low, popping a red balloon. But Brad's dart popped the white balloon. I closed my eyes and accepted defeat.

"Well done, Sir."

"Thank you my Lady."

A couple minutes later, the booth attendant sat a blue plastic sword and a sparkly, fluffy, purple unicorn the size of a small pony on the counter.

Brad lifted the unicorn and held it out to me, "For you."

"I thought you wanted it."

He shrugged, "I'll find something else for my niece."

"Keep it, it would just get put on a shelf in my house anyway." I lifted my sword. "This, on the other hand, is going into my next costume."

I pushed a button and the sword made a swishing sound.

"Zoey will be very happy, my sister on the other hand, less so. Thank you."

"I didn't know you had a sister."

"She's the best little sister. We had our moments growing up. She was constantly getting me in trouble. She dropped out of college to raise Zoey and my parents cut her off because they didn't approve of her husband. He died on deployment and I moved back here to help her with Zoey as much as I can."

"That must be really hard."

"She's a fighter, and Zoey is the smartest first grader I've ever met."

"Does she like sparkly unicorns?"

"*Like* is an understatement. She has unicorn pajamas, enough toys to fill her closet, a lunchbox, and a tea set. They're her favorite animal, and sparkly purple is the 'bestest' color ever according to her."

It was easy to tell from the way he talked about her, and some of his patients, that he'd be a great dad someday. I smiled, and tried to imagine Brad with a kid of his own. His hazel eyes, and dark hair like mine.

"She's lucky to have an uncle like you then."

"Yeah, Kim probably sees it another way. I've filled their house with toys galore. I might be spoiling her just a bit."

"If you babysit, I doubt she'd protest the unicorn."

"Great idea. I'll have to take it over tomorrow when I watch Zoey."

We weaved our way out of the festival and were headed back to Brad's car when a reporter for the local paper stopped us.

"Brad, are you loving the bidding frenzy that's likely to occur for you at the ball?"

Brad smiled professionally at the man. "I look forward to helping the Fire Station get the much needed funding."

"On the festival's website, attorney Lindsey Stone states that no one will outbid her for you at the ball. Do you look forward to seeing your ex-fiancé again?"

The muscle in Brad's jaw clenched as he replied, "No comment."

After a few more *No comments,* from Brad, the reporter took a picture of Brad with the unicorn and walked away.

We were quiet as we finished the walk back to his car. He placed the unicorn in the back, it sprawled across the entire back seat.

"Ex-fiancé?" I asked when we were both inside the car.

He sighed, and finished clipping his seatbelt. "Lindsey was not who I thought she was."

"Is she one of the women only interested in your money that you told me about?"

"Lindsey has only ever had two goals in life. One, to be at the top of society, and the second to marry better than her mother did. She cared more about who my parents were, than she ever cared about me."

His ex reminded me of a lot of things I'd heard Courtney's fiancé say. He was constantly telling my family at our family dinners about how his parents had risen through society and now belonged to the most exclusive country club on the east coast. He constantly name-dropped celebrities he'd met there.

"How long were you together?" I asked.

"We dated when I was in medical school. She was in law school so we didn't see much of each other. She'd planned our entire wedding with my Mother while I was surviving residency, even picked out her ring and how I would propose. I went along with it because it was easy to."

"How did it end?"

"When my sister called me from the bachelorette party to tell me Lindsey was leaving with a guy from the restaurant."

"I'm so sorry, Brad."

"I'm just glad she's not going to win the auction."

"Not if I have anything to do with it."

"My bank is mailing a card for you to use, it'll be here in five to ten business days." He started the car and pulled out of the stall.

"Speaking of the ball. Your mother said it was a masquerade. How much of a costume are we talking about?"

"Um..."

"Is it, wear a formal dress and slap on a mask? Or do I get to wear the whole fancy costume dress?"

"You could show up as a tortoise, and I'd be happy so long as you were there."

"I'm just realizing how big of a thing this ball is. The reporter took your photo, which means there'll be photographers at the ball too."

He nodded. "Want to risk more photographers and come back here with me tomorrow?"

He drove the car out of the parking lot and onto the main road.

As we left the festival behind I asked, "Will there be more cider donuts involved?"

"Absolutely."

"Count me in." I'd have to take a raincheck on running with Sofie.

# Chapter Six

When Brad had asked me to join him for the festival the next morning, I hadn't realized the first thing on the agenda was a sunrise hot air balloon ride. Needless to say, but I hadn't spent a lot of time getting ready that morning. Instead I'd rushed and put my hair into a messy bun, threw on a fuzzy sweater with jeans and called it good. Makeup was not even on my radar that early in the morning.

The sun wasn't up yet when we pulled into the parking lot next to the large field where hot air balloons were being set up. When Brad opened the car door for me to step outside, the cold autumn air made me want to duck for cover.

I shivered.

Brad reached into his backpack, and pulled out a thermos. "Apple cider as promised."

"Technically you promised donuts, but it's cold so I'll give you a pass."

He pulled out a donut in response. I grabbed the thermos to warm my hands and eagerly unscrewed the lid for a drink. The cinnamon apple flavor glided over my tongue, and the drink warmed me from the inside out.

"Thank you." I replaced the lid on my drink, and took the donut.

We strolled past several balloons before reaching a hot air balloon decorated in images of the Ice Princess.

"No way!" I stared at it in amazement.

One of the men setting up the balloon shook hands with Brad. "I'm Peter. We'll be ready in a few more minutes. Is it just the two of you?"

Brad nodded. "Thanks for doing this for me. I know it was a last minute request."

I gave Brad a questioning look.

"I saw a flyer at the cosplay run booth. I wanted to make it up to you for my rude comments."

"That's very thoughtful of you. As long as I don't die from this, consider it made up."

Peter took the opportunity to pipe up. "It's perfectly safe I assure you."

I studied Peter. "How long have you been flying balloons?"

"Fifteen years. Riding the wind is the best feeling in the world. Not knowing where you'll land, there's a freedom to that."

I looked at Brad in alarm.

"They have a car picking us up to bring us back here."

I nodded. "I won't freeze?"

"The basket is warmer than you think since we're close to all that hot air," Peter said. "I can control how high we go and I have some extra jackets in the basket if you need it."

I let out a squeak. "How high?"

Flying in an airplane was one thing, there were seatbelts and engines and I didn't have to look out the window. I looked at the wicker basket of the balloon in alarm. Was the thing safe? What if the balloon ripped? The thoughts raced through my mind, and I could feel panic rising like a tidal wave about to crash over me. Heights were something I did not do well with.

Brad squeezed my hand in concern, "If you don't want to do this, you don't have to. I'm afraid of heights, but I'll do it if you will."

I looked at my superhero on the balloon. She was fearless and beautiful. Facing her fear in a ball gown covered in icicles she used like throwing knives. I could face my fear of heights too.

"No, I'll do it."

I drank my cider and Brad ate a donut while we waited for the balloon crew to finish preparations. Before I knew it I was inside the basket with Brad and Peter. Brad held his arms around me, and I wanted to bury my face in his jacket.

Peter let out a jet of fire into the balloon, the ground crew let go of the ropes, and we were airborne.

I squeaked and buried my face in Brad's jacket, like I'd thought about doing earlier. He was strong, warm, and smelled really good. With my eyes closed I didn't notice how far the balloon rose. I was lost in the comfort of Brad's arms. I don't know how much time passed when I felt him let out a long breath.

I lifted my head and peeked through my lashes. The sky was brightening, gold stretched across the clouds. I loosened my hold on Brad, and he loosened his on me so I could turn for a better look. We were caught between the light and dark of a new day. Stars winking out, as the sun took over the sky.

"It's beautiful," I whispered.

"It's amazing." Brad whispered back, his breath warm on my ear.

We didn't say another word as we watched night colors pass into day. We just hovered in the air, taking in the view as the wind had paused.

Peter pointed out a few landmarks, before the wind began to gently push us. Our guide found a field to land in, and I felt Brad's hand tighten on mine. I looked at him, and saw that he'd paled.

"Are you alright?" I asked.

He squeezed his eyes shut. "It's always the landing that gets to me. I can't even watch my plane land."

I hugged him, and felt his arms slide around me in return. "I'll tell you when it's over."

I didn't dare watch the ground, instead I watched Peter as he competently controlled the descent.

"Brace yourselves," Peter said.

I shifted my feet to widen my stance, and bent my knees just a bit. Brad shifted as well, and his arms squeezed me tighter. I barely felt the basket jolt as it landed on solid ground. Brad wobbled, but not enough to fall over. Which was a good thing since we'd have both toppled.

"We did it." I couldn't keep the smile out of my voice.

Brad's eyes opened, and he smiled in return. His gaze traveled to my lips, and the warmth in my cheeks had nothing to do with the air in the balloon. He started to tilt his head down towards me, and I held my breath, waiting for his kiss.

"It was great to have the both of you." Peter slapped a hand on Brad's shoulder from behind.

Brad and I jolted apart. The romantic moment shattered as easily as a glass vase.

I cleared my throat and thanked Peter, before he walked away to start cleaning up the balloon.

A range rover and truck with a trailer pulled up, and our hot air balloon experience was officially over.

The driver chatted with us on the drive back to Brad's car. Asking if we'd enjoyed the experience and asking if we'd leave a review online. I let Brad chat, offering a word here and there. Mostly my thoughts were stuck on how it had felt to have Brad wrap me in his arms during the scary parts. Somehow it wasn't as frightening with him there. In fact it felt pretty wonderful, and I'd been happy to return the favor on the landing.

All too soon we were back in Brad's car. The giant unicorn still sat in the back seat. I hadn't noticed it when he picked me up as it was dark and I was tired.

"Didn't want to leave home without it?" I asked.

"Just decided there was no point in leaving it at my house, when I plan on heading to Kim's after helping with the pie bake off."

"What kind of pie?"

"I'll find out when I get there. I didn't have a lot of time between patients when Jack called to ask if I could come today."

"What time is the contest?" I looked at the clock to see it was nine-thirty now.

"Eleven. But I wanted to take a gift to Courtney's

wedding, so I was hoping we could look through the booths and find something."

"You don't have to do that. I already bought them a nice vase from their registry. I'd planned on signing both our names to the card."

He looked at me and frowned, before looking back at the road.

"I was raised to have better manners than that. But we can find something to go along with the vase so it looks like we picked both out."

"Okay." I'd long ago learned to let people buy things if they insisted, even if I didn't agree with it. He could decide what he spent money on, and I admired him for thinking of Courtney when he hadn't needed to.

He pulled into the same parking lot as the night before so we could wander around. The thought of checking out the different wares made me excited. There'd probably be one or two that I'd want to invite to the next comic convention in the area. Local artisans were a mixed bag, but it was easier to get community council approval if the town's businesses and people were excited about things.

I pulled my purse from under my seat and checked to see how many business cards I had.

The morning atmosphere was relaxed, while still holding an air of excitement. I hadn't realized how many vendors were at the festival the night before. Long rows of booths were set up all around the festival grounds. So many different types of vendors and I could happily spend hours looking at all of them.

We wandered through them taking in the trinkets, food, and hand crafted items.

I purchased a few fall scented candles from one vendor only to turn around and buy handmade soaps from another. A woman old enough to be my grandmother sold scarves she'd hand crocheted. Her grandson helped her run the card reader when I purchased a forest green scarf.

Brad purchased a delicate black and white scarf.

I lifted a brow in question. It was a nice scarf but I didn't think it was really a gift for a wedding.

"I need something to soften my sister up when she sees the unicorn."

I chuckled, and we continued to walk through the rows. I listened while he told me about Zoey's antics the last time he'd watched her. I shared some of my babysitting horror stories from when I was a teen.

Eventually we found a booth with a table runner that matched the color scheme on Courtney's registry. The stitching matched the color of the porcelain vase I'd purchased for her months ago. We also found a couple of candle holders that would go well with it.

The items were wrapped up, just in time to judge the pie contest.

The stage had long tables set up in a single row across it. That was the first sign that this wasn't a normal pie bake off. The second clue, was the wall of pies behind it.

"What kind of pie contest did you say it was?" I asked.

An announcement over the loudspeaker answered for Brad.

"The Bachelor Ball Pie Eating Contest starts in ten minutes."

Brad looked at me alarmed. "Let's make a run for it."

But it was too late. A hand clapped onto Brad's shoulder. The man had broad sculpted shoulders, brown hair, and was clean shaven.

The man grinned as he greeted us. "So good to see you Brad. Thank you for helping out the fire station."

"It's all for a good cause," Brad said, less enthusiastically. "You didn't mention it was a pie eating contest when you called."

"I made sure your pie is an apple one, don't worry.

"Who's this lovely lady?" the man asked.

Brad introduced me to his friend Jack, a member of the local fire station.

Other men began to sit at the table on the stage. Some dressed in dark blue shirts that said Police across the back, others wore red with the words Fire Fighter across the chest. A charged banter was exchanged between the two groups, but I couldn't tell what was being said, only observe the tension in their bodies as they spoke to each other.

Jack ushered Brad away from me so they could take their seats on stage. Brad was handed a matching firefighter shirt, which he slipped over his own. The gathering crowd cheered as the host took up the microphone. A screen on either side of the stage lit up, and video of the stage popped up. What I'd dismissed earlier as speakers or lights, actually held cameras so the audience could watch the pie disappear from multiple angles.

I quickly found a seat a few rows from the stage to observe the shenanigans about to go down.

"Ladies and Gentlemen, thank you for being here. We are about to witness the pie battle to end all pie battles. Chrissy's Bakery donated the pies for today. The town's finest bachelors from the bravest of the brave sit up here at this table. I think I speak for all of us when I say I hope they had the calendar shoot before now."

Laughter rippled through the crowd along with a couple whistles. Brad's eyes were large as he looked at his friend to confirm if there would be a calendar.

The host continued speaking. "To my left, in blue are the dedicated police officers that serve our fine community and ensure the donuts are safe. On my right, are the brave firefighters that fearlessly save cats stuck in trees."

Brad looked at me, the surprise of being entered into a pie eating contest, and possible photoshoot, finally wearing off. He winked at me, but it was the woman in the front row that giggled and waved at him in return.

I shrugged at her response, and gave him a thumbs up and a smile.

Assistants set a pie in front of each bachelor.

"The rules are simple, folks. First bachelor to finish his pie wins the donation from Chrissy's Bakery for their department. Not all of the fifty pies are for the bachelors to eat. They are also being sold and one hundred percent of the proceeds from today's sales will be donated to the winning department."

The host rattled off where to find the booth for the bakery for people to buy pies and other goodies. The rest of the rules were pretty standard. Hands had to be kept behind their backs and couldn't be used. At the end of ten minutes, if no one had finished the pie, three judges would determine the one who'd eaten the most and declare him the victor.

"When the bell chimes gentleman, get eating. When it

chimes again, times up." The host lifted his hand and dropped it when the chime sounded. "Eat Pie!"

The men smashed their faces into their pies, vigorously chewing. I looked across the bachelors and started to laugh. The police bachelors had been given blueberry pie, while the firemen had apple pies. It was pie carnage, as the sticky pie and whip cream smeared across their faces while they ate.

I hoped they had something for them to clean up afterward, because they'd have blue faces otherwise.

The officer who'd been instigating the charged banter glared at Brad's friend and I wondered what else had happened between them. Jack paused his eating to grin mischievously at the officer, and I thought the cop was going to start yelling.

"Five minutes!" The host shouted.

The officer went back to eating the pie, and so did Jack. Brad started to look a bit queasy and I wondered if all the sugar from the donuts, cider, and pie were going to do him in. He wasn't the only one though, several of the bachelors had slowed down.

"It's close folks. These fellas know how to eat. Let's cheer them on."

Jack and the officer ate with a renewed vigor as the assistants watched closely. The camera angles on the screen changed and the screen on the left zoomed in on the officer's pie, while the screen on the right zoomed in on Jack.

"Go Jack!"

I turned and saw an older firefighter had yelled it from the audience. He got the firefighters near him to start chanting Jack's name.

"One minute!" The host declared

As the crowd chanted, Jack continued to eat pie. More and more of the pie tin became visible. But the officer wasn't slowing down either. I couldn't tell by looking at the screens who would win.

"Ten seconds!" The host counted down and the crowd did too.

The screens changed again, this time to show a view of the entire table.

"One!"

The bell sounded and Brad and the others leaned back in their chairs. Three judges walked by the table to look at the pie tins and declare the winner. The judges shook their heads at the host.

"Ladies and gentleman, this is exciting. None of the contestants finished their entire pie tin. Our judges have not been able to tell visually who has eaten the most pie. We've got to bring out the scale."

The pie assistants brought out a food scale and held it up before setting it up in the center of the table. They picked up the officer's pie tin and Jack's pie tin. A cameraman walked onto stage to project the footage directly on the screens. The first tin was set on the scale and I watched as the numbers slowly settled. The officer's tin held a few pieces of crust and blueberries.

Jack's pie tin also had some crust and apple chunks and I could see why the judges hadn't been able to tell just by looking at it who won. They placed his tin on the scale and the crowd was silent. Only the sounds from the booths and rides around the festival could be heard as the numbers on the scale bounced high, then lowered one by one.

# Chapter Seven

When the final number flashed to signal the weight, the cheer from the firefighters could have rivaled any siren.

"The firefighters win!" The host called across the mic.

Brad slapped Jack on the back, as the other firefighters rushed him.

The host kept talking over the celebration. "Remember where to get your pies folks. It's all for a good cause. To donate to the town's finest, go to the fall festival website. You'll find the details for the officer's silent auction, and the firefighter's bachelor auction."

Pictures were taken of the pie eaters, before and after they were given wipes to clean their face.

By the time Brad exited the stage, the crowd had thinned. A woman with a short blond bob, met him at the bottom of the stairs. She blocked his path, and his expression was one of shock as he looked at the woman. I hurried towards him so I could be close if he needed me.

Brad reached for me as I got close, and wrapped an arm around my waist. He pulled me tight to his side, and I looped my arm around him. Together we faced the beautiful woman. She was dressed in custom tailored clothes from the latest fall fashion catalogue. Jeans off of a rack would not have fit that well over her leather boots. Neither would a commercial vest have wrapped along her curves to enhance her tiny waist instead of making her torso look boxy.

I felt Brad's lips brush the top of my head quickly in an affectionate kiss. Nerves in my stomach fluttered to life. This was one person Brad did not want to know we were faking it.

"Lindsey," Brad said. "Can I help you?"

The woman looked at me, appraising my worth with a quick glance up and down. For a moment I regretted not putting more time into my appearance for the day. I was not dressed like a fashion magazine model, like this woman. But, I'd learned over so many years at conventions it didn't matter what costume people wore. All that mattered was their character.

If Brad hadn't already told me the type of person she was, I wouldn't have needed him to tell me. She was like a beautiful painting of a fire. Beautiful to look at, but at the end of the day cold, and lacking realness.

She smiled at him like a wolf at a lamb. "I just wanted to let you know I'll be wearing a white dress to the ball so we can coordinate our outfits for the photos."

Brad shook his head. "I don't need to know that. Nor do I want to."

"With all the publicity surrounding the auctions, I'm sure the paper will be taking photos of us dancing."

Putting on my best imitation of Courtney, I made sure

to look her up and down like she wasn't worthy. She definitely wasn't deserving of a wonderful person like Brad. Anger sparked in me at her actions, she'd played with Brad's heart, broke it, and then waltzed up to him with the audacity to demand his attention at the ball.

I put on a cold smile of my own. "I'm afraid his dance card is full."

Lindsey glared at me, before turning back to Brad. "I'll pass on my dress information to Evelyn while we're eating lunch tomorrow. I know your mother always takes care of your tux."

"My mother doesn't control who I date, or dance with."

"No, but she does control the Ball, and I'm going to win that auction." Her red lips tipped into a smirk as she looked at me. "Not that it's hard to outbid all the bargain bin brats around here."

The urge to punch her in her perfect nose was strong, but I resisted. It wouldn't matter what Brad or I said to her here. But I worried how much she'd pay. I didn't know how much Brad was putting on that card, but from the designer purse hanging on Lindsey's shoulder, I'd bet she was going all in.

I lifted my free hand and rested it on Brad's chest where it said Fire Fighter in block lettering. His shirt was sticky from some pie that had fallen on it.

"I'm sure the fire fighters will appreciate any donation they receive. If it wasn't for such a good cause, I wouldn't even consider letting my boyfriend dance with desperate women. But I do believe in being charitable to those less fortunate than I."

Brad's chest moved under my hand as he took a deep breath. Inwardly, I cringed at phrasing it so it sounded like Brad was my property to loan out. No one should be demeaned in such a manner. But people like Lindsey only saw others as objects to be used to their advantage, or disregarded like garbage.

Her glare turned colder. "I'll call you later, Brad."

Then she turned and stomped away.

I peeled my hand off of his shirt, my fingers sticky from the pie. I was almost afraid to know what Brad thought of what I'd said. While I debated with myself if I should apologize or explain myself, he began to laugh. A deep, chest rumbling, tears forming kind of laugh.

Jack joined us. "Was that Lindsey?"

I nodded, and looked at Brad.

Jack asked him, "I've never seen her stomp away like that. What did you do?"

Brad pointed at me. "She made it sound like a pity dance for whoever wins me at the auction."

Brad broke out into more laughter, and Jack joined in. I was the one left in the dark.

"You're not mad?" I asked Brad.

He shook his head. "I've never seen her so ruffled. The most I've ever gotten out of her were fake smiles, and a shrug when I told her the wedding was off."

"The station is going to get so much money at the ball. There's no way the police will win the auctions with Lindsey bidding on you." Jack's smile was so big it looked like it was going to split his face. He turned to me. "Now she's going to drive the bid up so ridiculously high just to prove she's earned it."

I looked at Brad in concern.

"Don't worry about it, there's plenty on the card. I'll just tell my accountant to add a couple extra zeros to the balance."

My jaw popped open. I knew he was a doctor, but how rich was he? He so casually talked about adding zeros.

"Welcome to the world of the rich and famous," Jack said in pity. "They'll never understand what it's like for the common folk."

Brad playfully punched Jack in the shoulder. "I'd rather write you a check and forget all this nonsense."

His words stung and I dropped my arm from around Brad so I could take a step back. I was part of the nonsense he was wrapped up in.

Jack must have realized how I'd taken what he'd said. "If I could pick anyone to have money it would be Brad. He's always trying to give it away to people that can't afford their hospital bills. He's one of the good ones."

Just like he'd taken care of my ankle.

Brad flushed a bit at Jack's praise. "Just remember that when I tell you that I got Luke and Scott to volunteer for the Ball too."

Jack swallowed hard, and nodded as he looked at the ground.

"They were a bit offended you didn't ask them directly," Brad said.

Shrugging, Jack replied, "They're busy."

"Not too busy for you. Expect a good ribbing at poker night."

There was more they both had to say, so I made an excuse to give them some time.

"I'm going to go wash my hands and check on the cosplay booth. I want to see which characters they have signing today. Congratulations Jack, on your win. Maybe next time you can tell me how you arranged the blueberry pies for the policemen."

They both laughed.

"Sure will."

I walked away and found a hand washing station not too far away. Aside from Lindsey, it had been a wonderful morning. Maybe Brad would consider keeping in touch after the ball. It didn't take much to imagine how well he'd fit in on movie nights with me and Sofie. Perhaps his friends could come over too. Jack was fun, and I knew one of his other friends had introduced him to comics.

As I thought through possibilities for the future, I weaved my way through the crowd to the cosplay booth. The line for the booth was thirty people long, which was a good sign. Marie and I had worked together to get local cosplayers to play characters at the booth. They helped to draw people to the booth, and for a small donation people could get their picture taken.

It took awhile to move through the line, and Brad had caught up with me by then. He'd removed the sticky firefighter shirt and looked like he'd washed up somewhere since his hair looked damp.

When Marie saw us, her face lit up. "Beth! I'm so glad to see you. I have a favor to ask."

"What is it?" I asked.

"I need characters for the pumpkin patch news spotlight next Saturday. I'm hoping it'll inspire more race signups."

"What about Zach and Gabby?"

They were scheduled to be a prince and princess for half the day.

Marie shook her head. "I've tried calling and texting about the costume fittings, but no answer. I can't risk it."

My mind began spinning through other cosplayers I knew. Zach and Gabby were typically reliable, and familiar with the con circuit. They were professional and I always got great reviews when they worked.

"I'll find someone by Monday. I'm so sorry."

I could see the stress on Marie's face as she looked at me and Brad.

"What about you? Do you still have that princess dress from the run last year?"

"Yes, I'd be happy to, but I thought you wanted a couple. You specifically asked me to find a couple to show the run was for everyone."

She turned to Brad hopefully. "You up for it? Prince Charmaine?"

He looked alarmed as he considered what she was asking. "I've never done that type of thing before. I'm not sure-"

"Beth can talk you through it. She'll be by your side the entire time." Marie pulled a measuring tape from her pocket and moved around the table. "I just need a couple measurements to make sure the costume fits."

Marie hummed to herself as she took his measurements and declared the costume would be ready for him the next Saturday. She gave him directions for where and when to meet her for the costume.

Later when we were by the car, Brad paused while opening the door for me.

"Does anyone ever tell Marie no?" He asked.

I shook my head. "I don't think so. But I've never quite been railroaded into something like that. I'll find someone to cover the event and call her Monday with the details."

He shook his head. "That's okay. I'd like to try it, see what it is you love about it."

"Are you sure?" I asked.

"I'm sure. Besides, I don't want to know what it would feel like to disappoint her."

# Chapter Eight

Later that evening I sat on the lumpy brown couch, not caring about my lumbar support as I savored every bite of the barbeque chicken pizza. Sofie had even splurged for the high quality pizza, adding pineapple on half of it since she knew I liked it. Sofie hated pineapple on pizza with a passion. This could only mean one thing. She was buttering me up so I'd spill the juicy details about Brad. I'd planned on giving them to her anyway, but I savored the chance to eat the pizza while it was still hot. Once we got started talking, I wouldn't be taking another bite until long after it turned cold.

Sofie hit play on the movie we'd watched every October since we were kids. I could quote it by heart, as the movie opened to reveal the sinister plot the witches had planned for the people of Salem.

"Spill," Sofie demanded, and handed me a small bottle of cold Dr. Pepper.

She lifted her own pineapple free slice of pizza to her mouth and ignored the movie.

I told her about all the things Brad and I had done over the weekend. She squealed over the hot air balloon ride to watch the sunrise. By the time I got to Marie manipulating us into the pumpkin patch spotlight Sofie had forgotten about her pizza.

My Dr. Pepper had warmed as I'd held it, but I took a drink anyway. "We're having fun. I couldn't ask for a better fake boyfriend."

"But why does it have to be fake?" Sofie threw her hands in the air. "This could be your happily ever after!"

"Neither of us are interested in something serious. We both agreed this is temporary."

"You can change it. I've read so many books that prove just that."

"The books you read are meant to end that way. This is real life." I set my drink down and took a bite of cold pizza.

"I don't believe it. He's literally going to be your Prince Charmaine Saturday. He's a modern day prince in real life here to sweep you off your feet."

"How do you figure that?"

"All the contemporary romance novels are about rich doctors. It's the modern day equivalent of the Regency romances with dukes or princes. He's your princely Dr. Charming, who swooped in to save you from the evil stepsister's wedding."

I rolled my eyes. "There's no talking sense into you when you're like this."

The sun rose in the movie. A symbol of the light overcoming the darkness as the witches were defeated. Closing credits began to roll as I cleaned up after myself. I moved to the kitchen so I could put the pizza in the fridge, and my plate in the dishwasher.

Sofie walked in. "Fine. You're in a fake relationship with the perfect fake boyfriend."

"Thank you." I threw my soda bottle into the garbage.

"I'm not finished." Sofie planted her hands on her hips. "You need to be a better fake girlfriend."

"I do not!"

"He's barely met your family. Don't you think your dad finds it strange he's never been to a family dinner? He told you about Lindsey so you were prepared to come face to face with her. Have you prepared him for Asher? Sure he's met Courtney and Victoria so he has a hint. But your future brother in law is awful."

While I thought about her words, she walked back into the TV room and came back with her plate and cup. She had a point, and it wasn't fun to come to that realization.

"Fine. I'll invite him to Sunday dinner next week."

Sofie nodded and finished cleaning up after herself. "And you'll need to be affectionate with him."

"We're plenty affectionate."

"If you're going to convince your dad that you're suddenly in love, you're going to need to lay it on thick. He's going to be watching your goodbye through the window, and he'll know it's all fake if there's no kiss."

The thought of kissing Brad had the soda bubbles in my stomach tickling. It was unnerving.

"That will not be necessary."

The look in her eyes made me fidget, and I changed the subject. "How's your next book review going?"

We both knew what I was doing, but she let me slide.

"The troll won't be able to argue this one. No one can say Tolkien's works are garbage."

"You're caving! You're reviewing a book that isn't a romance."

"I am not. Tolkien's books have great love stories in them. My blog is pointing out that the greatest works are the greatest because of true love."

"The Book Beast got to you. He finally got to you. What will the book club ladies say?"

"That I should have another cookie." Sofie walked to her fridge. She opened the little door for her freezer to reveal dozens of bags full of cookies.

"Since when do you bake?" I asked, and snatched a bag of chocolate chip cookies for myself.

She groaned. "I don't! The ladies feel so bad about the Beast that they've been smothering me with cookies. I started freezing them when it became difficult to button my pants."

"Just leave them in your break room for the other librarians."

"I can't! My boss has already talked about shutting the blog down. Cookies lead to questions, questions mean that my boss will find out how much the comments bother me. He'll hand the blog off to someone else."

"Would that be so bad? Random comments from a stranger shouldn't bother you this much. Strangers don't know how awesome you are. Also no one recommends books as well as you do, and blog or no blog that'll never change."

"The blog is my baby. I had to fight for a year to get the approval for it. I can't just hand that off to someone else."

I reached for her hand and squeezed it. "Want me to see if Sebastian can get one of his web developer contacts to track down the Beast?"

She shook her head. "No thank you."

"I hate to say it, but I'd better get home."

"Go. Take some cookies to smuggle to your dad. I know Victoria has him on that strict diet."

I frowned. "I don't know why he puts up with it. He's always been a steak, potatoes, and dessert kind of guy. Now all of a sudden she says, no fat, no salt and he does it. I didn't realize all his meals were so bland until I moved back in for a couple weeks. I'll have to put the cookies in his study and hope she doesn't find them."

We said goodbye and I drove to my dad's house. Only a few short weeks and I'd get to sleep in my own house again.

<h1 style="text-align:center">Chapter Nine</h1>

Sunday afternoon blew in with a rain storm. The temperature dropped lower than before. I sat in my bedroom at the window seat, wrapped in a quilt while I watched the rain fall. Leaves fell from the trees, reminding me of the storm the night before I'd met Brad. The urge to run again hit me hard. It had been almost a week since I'd met him. I'd followed his directions and my ankle felt a little tight, but hadn't felt sore in days.

All the walking at the festival hadn't seemed to bother it one bit. I pulled out my phone to text Brad.

*Me: Can I run yet?"*

*Brad: Any pain?*

*Me: Nope.*

*Brad: Ease into it. Want to run together?*

I had not expected that, but it was convenient to test out running with a doctor as my jogging partner.

*Me: I'd love to.*

*Brad: Meet you at 7AM at our bench.*

The smile that spread on my lips was one hundred

percent a result of the joy in my soul. It felt like being in high school and getting asked to a dance all over again. I reminded myself to take Sofie's advice, embrace my girlfriend cosplay, this was the feeling I needed to show my dad at Sunday dinner. I'd invite him when I saw him tomorrow.

A knock sounded on my bedroom door. My dad poked his head inside.

"Time for dinner, Beth."

As I looked at him, I saw the exhaustion on his face. He'd aged while I'd been out living my life, and I hadn't realized how much until now. I unwrapped myself from the quilt and walked over to give him a hug.

"What's this for?" he asked, as he returned the hug.

"I love you, Dad."

He smiled, and the wrinkles on his face lifted. "I love you too, Bethy. Your mother would have loved to see you grown and in love."

"She knew I loved you."

The hug ended, and he chuckled as he patted my shoulder. "It's not me I was talking about."

We walked downstairs to the dining room together. Victoria, Courtney, and Asher were seated at the table waiting for us. The table was set with fine china and crystal glasses. Trays of food were arranged along the sunflower table runner in the middle. It looked like we'd be having fall vegetables and chicken for dinner.

"Sorry to keep you waiting," I said.

I slipped into my chair across from Courtney, while my dad took his chair at the head of the table opposite Victoria. Victoria drank from her glass at one end of the table, while Courtney sat next to Asher along the long side. Asher grunted, and continued typing on his phone, like he normally did.

Courtney cleared her throat. "Asher honey, can you put your phone away?"

He kept tapping as he said, "Yeah, I just gotta finish this."

My father exchanged a concerned glance with Victoria. As the dinner progressed, my dad and Victoria did most of the talking. Asher kept checking his phone, barely eating anything. Not that I blamed him, the vegetables had no seasonings. The chicken was bland and dry. Victoria had banned any type of sauce long ago. I'd resorted to using a lemon slice meant for my water to add some flavor. Courtney's body language grew more tense each time she whispered to Asher and he ignored her.

I sighed as I thought of my childhood Sunday dinners with pot roasts and mashed potatoes doused with butter and gravy.

"Is everything alright?" Victoria asked.

Not wanting to hurt her feelings, I decided to bring up the topic of inviting Brad over.

"I was just thinking I'd like to invite Brad for dinner next Sunday. Maybe we could have a pot roast?"

Victoria looked stunned, and I worried I'd hurt her feelings anyway. I looked at my dad to see him beaming.

"Who's Brad?" Asher asked, and set his phone down by his plate.

"Her boyfriend. He's her date to our wedding. I told you about it at lunch Wednesday." Courtney looked flustered.

Asher shook his head, and in a patient patronizing tone

said, "No you didn't. I would have remembered something like that. Now I have to tell my parents they'll need to pay to add one to the rehearsal dinner seating."

Courtney's brow creased as she thought about it. "I thought I'd told you. No need to worry your parents. He's her plus one, and was counted into the guest list all along."

"What about Easton? He's supposed to sit by Beth."

"The wedding planner and I have him sitting next to Samantha. I think they'll get along well."

"He's my best man, you can't move him to another table!"

Asher grew angrier, a fist clenching on top of the table where it rested near his plate. Courtney grew quieter as he told her how upset his family would be. How the day was supposed to be perfect and now it wasn't going to be.

"Asher," Victoria interrupted his rant. "Easton is still sitting at the table with the wedding party. I can show you the seating arrangement after dinner."

He turned to stare at Courtney. "Why didn't you just say so?"

"Asher." My dad's tone was stern. "A word in my study. Now."

My dad left the table, Asher huffed and then followed. Courtney looked like she was about to cry. I looked at Victoria to see that she was pinching the bridge of her nose.

"Please tell me he doesn't treat you like that all the time," I said to Courtney.

"It's the wedding stress. He's been working overtime so he can take time off for the honeymoon. It'll be better after the wedding. You'll see." She stirred the squash medley around her plate.

Several minutes passed, and we waited in a tense silence for the men to return to the table. My father entered first, and took his seat.

Asher stood in the doorway and cleared his throat. "I guess I should say I'm sorry. I regret that you all got upset. I have strong opinions and I was just trying to help my cousin feel welcome at the wedding."

Courtney smiled at him. "Of course I want Easton to feel welcome."

Victoria and my dad mumbled words of agreement about wanting his family to be comfortable. Something didn't feel right, but I couldn't quite put my finger on it. Instead, I nodded to Asher and the rest of the family and excused myself. It didn't take long to clean up my dishes before I headed up to my room.

As I tried to fall asleep later that night, I hoped Courtney was right and that Asher was just stressed. I thought of Brad and wondered how he would have reacted. Sofie was right, again, Brad needed to be warned about family dinner with my future brother-in-law.

# Chapter Ten

Sofie was putting all her energy into her next blog post and skipping her runs with me as a result. I ran every morning that week with Brad. My ankle had made a full recovery, and we trained for the cosplay run together. It was amazing how well we were able to keep pace together.

That was how I found myself with extra time to finish the alterations on my bridesmaid dress, and finish all of my work. My boss Sebastian and I were on our weekly video call as I typed up notes on what he wanted for the spring convention.

My foot tapped under my desk as I told him, "I've been able to secure half of the desired actors for the convention. The agencies for the other half are being difficult. They blame filming conflicts and contractual obligations. I don't think they realize I have their co-stars from Fire Storm already signed."

Sebastian threw a stress ball up in the air and caught it over and over again as he sat in his private office. I'd been to his ornate home office a few times before he decided that technology was more convenient. Through my computer screen I saw that the sun was streaming through the large glass windows behind him, and the large bookshelves were still full of the leather bound volumes.

I'd once told Sofie about his book collection of first printings, and other collectible books. She'd begged me to convince my boss to let her take a look, but I hadn't asked him yet as the timing wasn't right. Yes, I knew my boss well enough he treated me like an adopted sister. We worked well over phone and email, since we couldn't be distracted as easily from the task at hand. Since he traveled so frequently, it also gave him the freedom to send me his ideas when they struck at one in the morning. The arrangement gave me the freedom to organize the chaos without killing his creativity.

These video calls were as much about talking business as chatting about our personal lives. He had always been an incredibly private person when it came to his personal space. Out of everyone at our company, I was the only one I'd known of that had been to his mansion. The decision to close our office had come as a shock to all of us as we thought he wanted to keep his personal and business separate.

"Go ahead and start the announcements for the current line up. I don't want to lose the ticket sales for holiday shoppers while we negotiate a couple contracts."

"Will do, boss. Anything else you need me to do?"

He set down the stress ball. "Yes. I want you to see what it would cost to put together a Regency event in the area next summer."

His words took me by surprise and I had to think for a moment about how to respond.

"You think it's a terrible idea." He leaned back in his chair and sighed. "Forget it."

"No," I said quickly. "It's just different from our normal market."

"I went to a tea and cake shop while I was in London. There was a table full of grown women giggling about their Jane Austen tour. There's an entire tourist industry there and it got me thinking."

"About?"

"I got into the comic convention industry because I like comic books. Why couldn't we expand our business to encompass other types of books too?"

"Excellent point. I'll see what information I can gather before our next meeting."

"Thank you, Beth. I'll see you next week."

"Actually it'll be two weeks. I have a Bridal Brunch next week for my stepsister."

"Sounds terrible."

"Sebastian, really."

"Have a lovely time discussing place settings and flower arrangements. Remind me to send something tacky from their registry."

"You don't know them."

He waved a hand. "She's your family, and you're my work sister. That basically makes her my sister."

I chuckled at his logic. "I'll never understand rich people. You would buy an evil stepsister a wedding gift. He offered to be my fake boyfriend. It's all too much."

Sebastian leaned forward in his chair. "Who did what now?"

I looked at my phone on my desk, to see a calendar reminder about my house. "Got another call. I'll see you in two weeks. Bye!"

I couldn't click the end call button fast enough on my computer. Sebastian was a great boss, and like he'd said, we were work siblings. We could tease each other mercilessly, but at the end of the day we had each other's back. He knew I didn't date, and I pretended I didn't read the tabloids with his picture in them.

A text popped up on my phone from Sebastian.

*Boss: Face to face in person next time. I'll supply the good stuff.*

He played dirty. The first time I'd tried the German chocolate bar he'd brought me I was hooked. I'd looked online everywhere for the brand so I could get my own supply. But I'd never had any luck, it was some super fancy brand that only elite guests of an exclusive hotel Sebastian stayed at could get.

*Me: Do you have a secret stash somewhere?*

*Boss: Yes. If you want it, come get it. I'm in town for a while for a thing.*

*Me: I expect a box of it.*

*Boss: No dice. You're making me wait and I know you lied about the call.*

*Me: How?*

*Boss: You're texting.*

I wanted to smack myself.

*Me: Fine, but I expect sandwiches from your chef. Flooring is going in at my house so I need to go.*

Thirty minutes later, I had my jacket on, phone in my purse, and keys in hand as I strolled from my car to the door of my house. The stone cottage had seen better days, but I loved how the ivy grew up a trellis near the brick chimney. My yard was small, and currently filled with the flooring crew waiting impatiently for me to open the door.

Inside, my house was sad, it smelled like dust and stagnant air. The original hardwood floors were gone due to the water damage. Plywood made up the floor, but I hoped that it would soon be a real floor again. I found the general contractor, to see how long it would be until I got my house back.

"Hi Georgie. How long do you think this will take?"

She looked at her clipboard and sighed. "Don't kill me."

"I don't like the sound of that."

"We only got half the order to the warehouse. We're still waiting on the rest of the order to arrive from Canada."

"Why is my flooring in Canada?"

She shrugged sheepishly. "Shipping mishap. We put a rush on it at no cost to you."

The crew brought in packages of flooring and then left. Georgie delivered the news that to get a better looking floor they needed all the packages before they began installing it. She opened a couple of the boxes to show me the gorgeous dark walnut planks. They'd contrast prettily with the white kitchen cabinets.

I looked at her. I trusted Georgie. She'd been frustrated every step of the way with me. From the hassle with the insurance adjuster, to the hold up on the flooring.

"Please tell me I'll be able to move my new furniture in before it snows," I said.

"I'll have it Monday. The supplier is paying to have it overnighted once it clears customs."

We left my house, and I locked my front door. "See you next week."

/ Chapter Eleven

Saturday morning dawned cold and clear. I wore my baby blue princess dress, that I'd sewed multiple layers of a sheer sparkly organza fabric over the top. The effect was eye catching in the sun or bright lights, as the dress shimmered in different shades of blue. I'd have to use the same stuff again when I made my Ice Princess dress. I filled my back pack with a change of clothes, wallet, and phone. Then I threw in safety pins, hair spray, glitter gloss and my travel make up for good measure.

Brad and I had opted to meet at the pumpkin patch since he'd be getting costumed up there. The drive took me maybe ten minutes, since traffic was light. The costume spotlight was scheduled to be filmed live during the morning news, so we needed to be early to go over what was expected of us.

I parked and then finished my costume by putting on long gloves and a sparkly gold tiara. The gravel crunched under my gold heels as I walked across the parking lot in search of Marie and Brad. Unsure of where to meet them, I texted Brad to let him know I'd arrived.

Ten minutes later I was stunned to see Brad walking to me. A modern Prince Charming in the flesh. He wore a white tuxedo fashioned after the renaissance period. Instead of a tie, his dress shirt had fancy gold buttons that matched his vest, coat, and cufflinks. The coat had gold embroidery that ran down the lapels, then down to the bottom of the coat tails. His black boots were polished to perfection.

He cleared his throat nervously.

"You're perfect." I shook off my daze and stepped closer to him. "Thank you so much for doing this. It means the world to Marie."

"She told me that repeatedly, but I still feel like a fish out of water."

Marie chose that moment to join us. "I've told him, smile and be courteous. That's all I need, the camera will do the rest."

"Excellent advice for having photos taken, I'm not so sure how it works for video."

She waved her hand in dismissal. "I'll be doing the majority of the talking to the reporter. I just need the two of you to look good, and if asked to talk about how fun it will be to run while dressed up."

"We can do that," Brad held out an arm for me to loop mine with, before holding out his other arm for Marie. "Shall we?"

While the patch was not packed, there were many families wandering the rows and piles of pumpkins. Children squealed in delight and laughed as they ran to look at all sorts of pumpkins. I saw big, small, white, orange, and even a few blue-green ones scattered throughout.

A little girl, who couldn't have been more than six, yanked on her mom's hand and pointed at us. She began jumping up and down in her purple princess dress. I waved like a pageant princess at her, and her smile was big enough to show all her teeth. She looked at her mom and began chatting excitedly.

The camera crew and reporter had us stand in front of a wall of hay bales and carved pumpkins.

Marie did wonderful as always in explaining the cause and need for donations to fund the research. As they spoke a small crowd gathered to watch. The little girl and her mother stood at the front of it, although her mom looked like she was trying not to laugh. The reporter asked his last questions for Marie and then turned to Brad and I.

He shifted the mic just a little and asked us, "Can we get a little preview of the race? I'm sure our community would love to see if the Prince or Princess would win."

Smiling through my response, I said, "I'm afraid I didn't wear my running heels this morning. But my fairy godmother assures me they'll be ready for the race."

The little girl's gasp was loud enough I thought the camera would pick it up. The reporter wrapped up his commentating, and told the camera how they could donate. The camera turned off, and we said our goodbyes to the reporter. Out of the corner of my eye, I saw the little girl getting closer, although her mother was trying to slow her down.

"Mom, she's a real princess with a fairy godmother!"

Brad turned to look at the girl and her mom. Groaning,

he rubbed a hand over his eyes. The mother started laughing and let go of the little girl's hand. She ran to Brad and hugged his leg.

"Tell Mom, Uncle Brad. She's a real princess."

"Zoey," her mom said. "Brad's not a real prince, they're just in costume."

Picking up Zoey, Brad asked her mom. "Why are you here Kim?"

"It's not everyday a blackmail opportunity falls in my lap." Kim lifted her phone and snapped a photo of Brad and Zoey.

"Mom, my headband!" Zoey frantically looked around at the ground.

"Right here." Kim pulled a sparkly purple headband with a unicorn horn on top of it out of her leather purse.

Zoey snatched the headband and put it on top of her head. "I'm a unicorn princess!"

"I thought you were going to be a mermaid for Halloween? You showed me your costume yesterday."

"What did you think would happen when you gave her the giant unicorn?"

Zoey stared at me. "Are you a real princess?"

I shook my head. "I'm not, I just like to pretend."

"Did you lie about your fairy godmother?"

Brad and Kim looked at me to see what I'd say.

"They don't use magic, but I like to think people like my friend Marie are fairy godmothers. Did you know Marie turned your Uncle Brad into a Prince just for the pumpkin patch?"

She looked at Marie with a skepticism in her gaze, before asking her. "Will the spell wear off after the ball?"

Marie laughed. "He can use it for the ball."

Brad shook his head. "Marie, that's too generous."

"Nonsense." She waved his concerns away. "In fact, keep it. I've barely had use for it since Beth started helping me organize cosplayers with their own costumes. Consider it a thank you gift for helping me today."

*Fairy Godmother*. I mouthed to Kim while pointing to Marie. Kim nodded vigorously in return, then pointed to her brother and mouthed back, *Prince Charming*.

Zoey hugged Brad tight. "You can go trick-or-treating with me now."

Kim laughed, Brad graciously accepted Marie's gift, and Zoey chatted away about all the candy she was going to get in her plastic pumpkin. Marie said goodbye and handed us wristbands to enjoy the pumpkin patch hayride and corn maze. She had to return to the festival booth down the street.

"Apple Cider donut?" Kim asked us, and pointed at the donut booth.

"Too soon," Brad groaned. "I can't look at an apple the same way after the pie contest."

Zoey forced Brad to set her down. "Donuts!"

Kim turned to me, "Donut?"

I shook my head. "No, I've had plenty lately."

While Kim and Zoey were getting donuts, a family asked Brad and I for a photo with their kids in knight costumes. Brad surprised me with how well he acted the part of a prince as he used one of their plastic swords to knight them for slaying the pumpkin dragon. For all his resistance to having a family, he would be a great dad.

His sister returned. "Let's head over to the hayride. The guy at the donuts said the line is long already."

Happy to spend time with Brad, I joined him and his family on the hayride, and to walk through the maze. Zoey and I talked about princesses and unicorns for most of the maze. I almost convinced her that the Ice Princess was the best princess, but Zoey argued only purple dress princesses were the best. Kim and Brad talked quietly together, although she teased him plenty too.

The day was perfect, and I realized that I'd had a lot of those with Brad.

Sunday dinner started off on a good note. Victoria had made a pot roast like I'd requested, much to my surprise. There were no buttery mashed potatoes though, just green salad, and dinner rolls.

Brad sat next to me at the table, and chatted with my Dad to his right. Well, Brad chatted, my dad grilled him about his job, family, and hobbies. Victoria and Courtney discussed details for the Bridal Brunch Wednesday. Asher tapped away on his phone for half the dinner, much to my relief. But when the dinner plates were cleared, and dessert was served he stopped Courtney from reaching for the whipped cream to top her strawberries.

"Babe, are you sure that's a good idea," he said.

She looked at the three strawberries on her little plate, and then passed the whipped cream to Asher. He smiled at her and proceeded to put a large dollop on his own plate. My dad frowned, but didn't take any of the cream after looking at Victoria, who smiled at him in relief.

The room felt uncomfortable to be in, and I wanted the night to be over.

I'd never understand the power she held over him when it came to food. Brad served himself the strawberries and cream, but didn't start eating like the others had.

I filled my own plate, piling it higher since I was the last to get the bowls for dessert. I ate the first bite, delighted with how the sweetness of the cream offset the tartness of the strawberries.

"The strawberries are delicious." My father told Victoria. "Your greenhouse is the best idea you've ever had, if we can eat these year round."

Brad scooped a single strawberry onto his clean spoon before swooping it into the cream. I'd noticed throughout dinner that he didn't take a bite of his own food, until after I'd started to eat my own. His manners were impeccable, and I found myself trying harder to eat like a lady. I wasn't a slob by any means, but I felt like one as I watched him elegantly glide his spoon towards his mouth.

He must have felt my stare because he looked at me before taking his bite.

"Beth," He looked amused as he smiled at me.

"Yes?" I asked.

"You have some of the cream on your nose."

I lifted my napkin quickly to wipe it away. "Did I get it?"

"No. It's just--" He moved to point out the spot on my face, but must have forgotten the spoon in his hand.

Before I could react, he booped my nose with his spoon. It was a light touch, and he started laughing. My dad joined in and then so did the others. I grabbed the spoon from the serving bowl and flicked it at him. A large splat of white hit his cheek. He wiped at it with his hand, looked at his covered fingers and then at me. He might not have meant to start a food fight, but I'd definitely escalated it.

"No throwing food at the table!" Victoria said sternly.

Sheepishly, I turned to her. "I'm sorry. I shouldn't have done that."

I cleaned my nose off in the bathroom and returned with a wet cloth for Brad to clean his cheek and hand. He'd wiped off the worst of it with his napkin.

Asher chose while I was out of the room to chat up Brad about investments.

"You may have noticed me on my phone tonight. I take my work seriously, and if you invest with me I'll work just as hard on your account as any other."

"What firm are you with?" Brad asked.

"Dawson and Sons."

Brad nodded. "I'm familiar with the firm. I've been pleased with the work Jim Dawson has done for me."

Asher paused, calculating his next move. "Mr. Dawson does very well. He is getting older though and needs to retire. You'll need someone new on your account, and I'm practically family."

Asher beamed at Courtney, then me.

Setting his spoon down, now that he was done with dessert, Brad said, "I'll think about it."

I wanted to melt into the floor.

"I'm sure you have a busy day tomorrow, Brad. Let me walk you out."

Brad thanked my parents for having him, said goodbye to Courtney and Asher, and we left. We were barely outside, with the door closed behind us, when I started apologizing for the disaster of an evening. In one evening

Brad had been interrogated by my father, smeared with food by me, and had to listen to Asher's sales pitch.

"It's fine, Beth." Brad assured me. "I've had worse dinners with my mother."

A curtain moved in the living room. "Ugh! And now my dad is probably watching us."

Brad stepped closer and wrapped his arms around me. I buried my face in his sweater, and the smell of his cologne calmed me. I could feel his silent chuckle as he held me tight.

I lifted my face to ask. "What's so funny?"

He leaned in and whispered in my ear. "I was just wondering if we should give him something to look at."

His breath was warm against the chilled night air. I shivered at the tingles that went down my neck, and my brain short circuited at what he was implying. We'd never discussed kissing. Why hadn't we discussed if we'd kiss in front of people.

Brad loosened his hold, and stepped away. The loss of his warm arms was as effective as dumping cold water on me. I hadn't said a thing, just stood there like a zombie while he held me.

"Goodnight Beth, I'll see you at our Bench tomorrow."

Our run together the next morning went as smoothly as all the runs we'd taken together had. My speed had picked up, and I felt like I'd be able to make a good time on the cosplay run at the end of the month.

As we stretched by our bench together, I noticed Brad staring at me. I'd caught him staring at me multiple times this morning.

"Do I have something on my face again?" I asked.

"No! I just have something to ask you."

I lifted a brow, "What is it?"

"What would you think about dating for real?"

Shock, stunned, flabbergasted. I opened my mouth to respond multiple times, but no words came out.

His shoulders slumped. "I shouldn't have sprang it on you like that."

"Why?" I asked. "I thought we'd decided that neither of us wanted a relationship."

"I've really enjoyed our time together. My reasons for not dating seem inconsequential now."

"I've enjoyed our adventures."

His eyes lit up with a spark of hope. "So. . . ?"

"I think I'd like to date you too." A giant grin spread across my face.

He let out a loud woop, lifted me up and spun me in a circle. I couldn't imagine anything better than the sweet joy that filled my heart. The perfect movie pizza night with Sofie couldn't come close. Not even meeting the Ice Princess come to life could have made me happier than I was now.

Brad made a part of my heart I thought long dead, beat again.

I still wore a smile days later. The smile only fading at Courtney's Bridal Brunch. Bridal Brunches had to be the worst idea in the world. I sat at a table of mostly strangers while we nibbled on fruit and scrambled egg whites. Even now Victoria controlled what Courtney and I ate. The caterer had provided a variety of mini muffins, and Victoria told us not to touch them.

Victoria sat at one table with the older guests. Courtney's future mother-in-law, aunts, and Victoria's friends that had been invited to celebrate Courtney's upcoming wedding. Courtney and I sat at a table with Courtney's maid of honor Samantha, and a couple of Asher's cousins. I couldn't remember their names, and it would be rude to ask at this point. There was an empty chair next to Samantha for another cousin that was running late. Sixteen people in total wasn't terrible, but the lack of familiarity was.

Courtney had dark circles covered with makeup, and mostly rearranged the food on her plate instead of eating it. Her friend Samantha looked green at the sight of the eggs and refused them. Instead she opted for the banana mini muffins and special ordered sparkling water from the kitchen. I ate my mixed berries in silence, while looking around at the venue.

It had possibilities for the Regency event Sebastian had asked me to look into. We were in a giant fancy green house of sorts, with views of the botanical gardens outside. The ground crew certainly knew what they were doing with the variety of vibrant fall colors complimenting each other. I could picture serving tea and cake, while the Jane Austen fans took a walk about the room or on one of the paths. Sofie would certainly go nuts over the idea, and she knew more about what sort of activities took place in the Regency era.

I was pulled out of my thoughts by the arrival of the last cousin. She took off her large tortoiseshell sunglasses, and smoothed her blond bob.

"Four days until the wedding," Lindsey said to Court-ney. "Are you still trying to lose weight so you fit in your gown?"

Courtney shook her head and took a sip of her water.

Lindsey frowned. "If you want the name of my personal trainer, I'm sure they could help you."

The other cousins offered their weight loss tips and I wanted to throat punch Lindsey. How dare she start picking on Courtney. Sure Courtney and I weren't best of friends, but that was mostly because Courtney focused on marriage and weddings. I wasn't interested in either of those things for myself and Courtney couldn't understand why.

I glared at Lindsey. "Her dress fits her perfectly, she's gorgeous."

"Well," Lindsey smiled, "It never hurts to lose a few pounds."

Courtney chuckled in an effort to break the tension. "Thanks Lindsey. I'll probably need the number after the wedding cake."

Samantha nodded. "I still can't believe you're doing chocolate cake with buttercream frosting."

"That sounds delicious." I took another bite of eggs.

Lindsey snorted and then turned to one of the cousins. "I have a friend getting married in Bali. She's flying the entire wedding party and guest list out. Destination weddings are the best, I can't believe people would choose anything else. It's your wedding, go big and fabulous I say. Anything else is for poor people."

Courtney flushed. Her and Asher were going to be married at the church, with the reception and dinner here. I looked at Courtney ready to open my mouth and say some-thing. Courtney shook her head, and the look she gave me pleaded for me to be silent.

As the brunch progressed, the cousins and Lindsey took

turns mocking everything about the venue, and wedding details Asher's mom had told them about. They agreed that it was all too cliché, the white roses, the chicken dinner, and especially the botanical gardens. Courtney was quiet, and her expressions became more controlled, until she gave off an indifferent, almost cold expression.

Samantha commented about how she'd heard Asher complain about the restraints of small town weddings.

"Excuse me." Courtney got up from her chair and gracefully hurried towards the door.

I didn't bother saying anything before going after her. I followed her to the powder room attached to the bathroom. Courtney was breathing hard, and staring at herself as she leaned against the counter under the ornate mirror. She started to mumble too quietly for me to hear.

She saw me in the glass, and sighed.

"Why do you put up with it?" I asked.

"It's not that bad, and they're right. I could have pushed for a trendier wedding."

"They're terrible people. "

Courtney shook her head. "No, they have certain expectations, and they want me to be better so that I meet his family's standards."

"I know I'm only a bridesmaid because our parents are married. But you need to be surrounded by people that love and support you."

She let out a short bitter laugh. "You're my bridesmaid because I didn't have anyone else. I don't have friends."

# Chapter Twelve

I had no words as I stared at her in astonishment. She'd been my stepsister for eight years, and in all those years I'd never really heard her talk about her friends. In high school she hung out with the popular crowd. Going to all the dances and games. Sofie and I had opted for movie marathons and pizza. Since she began dating Asher her sophomore year of college, Courtney only talked about the dinners and golf dates with Asher and his friends.

"What about Samantha?" I asked.

"We work together. She's helped with the wedding plans because she saw me botching it on my lunch break."

"The bachelorette party she threw you last month?"

"Didn't happen. I booked a hotel room for myself and got room service."

"Why?" I asked.

She sniffed and reached for a tissue from the counter to dab at the corner of her eyes. "I didn't want to admit my life isn't as perfect as I thought it was going to be. Asher's family treats me like a stray dog they've taken pity on. I didn't want to admit to them that I didn't have friends when they asked who would be in the bridal party. I had to bribe Samantha into being my maid of honor, since I knew you'd make it no secret we aren't close."

"I thought you hated me."

"Since meeting me and my Mom, you've treated us like we were stealing your dad from you. So maybe at first I did. I was jealous of how much people loved you, and how you are authentically you. I can't do that, all I can do is shop and max out my credit cards. You've made a career out of something you love, and don't care what people think about it either. All you needed was Sofie and your dad to be happy. You've never needed or wanted me."

Shame burned my cheeks, she was right. I hadn't been welcoming to her or her mom. I hadn't wanted more family, I only wanted my mom and Dad. My mind began whirling with ideas on how to broach the gap between us.

"I'm so sorry Courtney. If you still want it, I'd like a chance to see if we can be true sisters to each other."

"Me too." She blew her nose with a new tissue.

"Are you free for the rest of the day?" I asked.

"Yes?"

"Great. We're having a pizza-movie-sister party."

"Oh I can't eat pizza, I'll never fit in my dress if I do."

"I'll make the alterations myself if you need them. But if I had to guess, I think you've lost weight since your final fitting weeks ago."

"When you and Brad get married, I hope things go much smoother for you. He's so nice to you, and the way he reacted to the whipped cream. I could never do something like that with Asher."

"Is everything okay with you and Asher?"

She nodded, and pulled some cosmetics out of her clutch. "It's just stress."

After she'd touched up her makeup, we returned to the brunch. We spent the rest of the time chatting about movies and pizza toppings, while we ignored the barbs Lindsey and the rest of the cousin threw our way. Samantha had grown quiet and spent the last half hour of the brunch texting on her phone or talking to Lindsey.

I still felt ashamed with how I'd kept Courtney and Victoria at arms length. The more we talked the more I realized what we had in common. While superheroes would always be my first preference for movies, the second most loved genre was romance. Courtney loved the holiday romance movies that aired on TV each Christmas season, and we had several favorites in common.

When the conversation turned and Courtney began asking me questions about Brad, Lindsey and the other women at the table turned their attention to me.

"How did you meet Brad Charmaine?" Samantha asked. "He's like Crestfield royalty."

"We were running the same path at the park."

The cousins looked at Lindsey in concern. The blond bombshell was back to glaring at me.

Samantha fanned herself with her hand. "That must be how he keeps in such good shape. The photos of him on the ball website are amazing. I really hope they make a calendar."

I really should look at the website, it'd been mentioned multiple times by people I knew. But I didn't see the point when the only one I planned to bid on was Brad.

"Don't you think it's false advertising for him to be one of the bachelors if he's seeing you?" Lindsey asked.

I shrugged. "He was looped into the auction business before we'd told a lot of people we were together."

Lindsey smiled like a shark circling for the kill. "The Brad I know would never portray himself as single if he was taken. He doesn't lie like that. What I think is that he's planning on being single by the dance."

Courtney swallowed her water wrong, and coughed to clear it out. A pit formed in my stomach, I had a feeling that Lindsey could sense lies like a shark could sense blood in the water. It was a very good thing Brad and I were dating for real now. Even if we hadn't had a chance for a proper date since our run Monday.

"I'm not sure why you care so much about my relationship with Brad. Seeing as how you ruined your chances with him years ago." I said, enjoying the flush of embarrassment on Lindsey's face. "Besides, if you really knew him, you'd know he'd do anything for his friend Jack."

"Enjoy it while you can. We both know it'll never work out in the long run." Lindsey spat out. She stood from the table and picked up her purse. "I have to get back to court, I have an important case to handle."

She left without another word, but I was left to my thoughts. I didn't know what our long term plans were now that we'd decided to date for real.

The rest of brunch went smoother without Lindsey there to stir up trouble. Courtney, bless her, had distracted me from my troubled thoughts with her passion for decorating. In the car, she even offered to help me when it came time to move back into my home, since she should be back from her honeymoon by then. I caught Victoria's smile in the rearview mirror as we drove back to the house.

Courtney and I spent the rest of the day watching cheesy romances, and eating pizza. Victoria even joined us for one of the movies, although she declined the pizza. There was still awkwardness at times, but it gave me hope that things would get better between us.

# Chapter Thirteen

Friday afternoon, I wanted to throw something at Asher's cousin Easton.

He purposely messed up the timing as we walked down the aisle at the rehearsal. The wedding planner made us walk it over and over. Even moving us to a side aisle to practice while the rest of the wedding party went on with the rehearsal. When she had us walk it separately, he miraculously didn't have a problem anymore. I really, *really*, hoped that he wouldn't be a problem at the wedding tomorrow.

Easton turned to me when the wedding planner stepped out of earshot. "I hear you have a boyfriend."

"Sure do." I checked my phone to see if Brad was done with work yet. He'd had a late call to help a sick kid. He hadn't wanted to make the worried dad wait until Monday for an appointment, or put the kid through the stress of an emergency room visit.

"I don't mind," Easton put a finger under my chin and tilted my face up so I was looking at him. "It's not like he's here."

I was going to be sick for so many reasons.

I slapped his hand away. "One, don't touch me. Two, don't be gross. And three, let me be clear. I have no interest in anything you can offer."

I walked to the wedding planner and advised her that I would not be walking with Easton tomorrow.

Asher and Courtney walked over to see what the problem was. After I'd explained, Courtney glared at Easton who was laughing with Asher.

Courtney looked at the wedding planner. "What are our options?"

"Babe," Asher laughed. "It's not that big of a deal."

Courtney looked at her fiancé furiously. "I told you he was a problem weeks ago, you said you'd handle it."

Easton rolled his eyes, "Don't be such a bridezilla."

Courtney glared at him, and then looked at the wedding planner. "I don't care how you do it, but I want Easton kept as far as possible from Beth."

The wedding planner frantically consulted her notes on her clipboard. Then she came up with a new plan. The wedding planner directed Asher and his groomsmen on how they'd walk in from the side, before Samantha and I walked down the aisle to the music leading up to Courtney's entrance with my dad. Asher was irritated at the change of plans, but he seemed to realize that Courtney meant what she said.

The rest of the rehearsal ran smoothly, and I was glad that Easton kept his distance. Asher's parents kept reminding us about the rehearsal dinner, and how the rehearsal was running late. It wasn't like I'd had a chance to forget after the first ten times they'd mentioned it. Asher's parents had paid for a reservation at the fanciest steakhouse in town.

While Courtney and Asher were talking to the priest, I took a seat in one of the pews. Samantha sat down a moment later, and we silently watched as Asher and Courtney went through an abbreviated version of the ceremony.

"She's so lucky," Samantha sighed. "Asher's amazing."

I held my tongue and checked my phone.

Samantha continued talking. "He's such a catch, I don't know why he'd settle for Courtney. She's as interesting as a turnip."

The wedding planner shushed Samantha, and she didn't say another word as we waited for Courtney and Asher to finish. I texted Brad when we were on our way to dinner, glad when he said he'd meet me there.

The steakhouse hostess led the wedding party to one of the private dining rooms. Tables were set up in a U-shape so that we could all see each other while we ate. Brad and I sat on one of the side tables with my dad and Victoria. Asher, and Courtney sat at the bottom of the U, while Asher's parents, cousin Easton, and Samantha sat on the other side table. A couple other tables were squeezed into the room for some of Asher's extended family from out of town to join us. I was grateful when I did not spot Lindsay among them.

Dinner started with a tossed green salad, and crab cakes. Then progressed into serving poached salmon, prime rib, or lamb based on the guest's preference. As the waitstaff cleaned up the empty dinner plates, a mic was set up on a stand in the open space at the top of the U for anyone making a toast or speech.

A waiter set a slice of cheesecake topped with a chocolate drizzle in front of me.

"Do I need to make a speech?" Brad asked me.

"Not unless you want to." I took a bite of the cheesecake.

He leaned closer as he whispered, "I'm guessing the guy at the table opposite us, is the cousin you wished to avoid?"

I looked briefly at Easton, who was openly glaring at Brad. When he caught my look, Easton's face changed from angry to what must have been his flirty apology face. With his fingers he formed a heart shape in front of his chest.

I rolled my eyes, and whispered back to Brad, "I thought I'd solved it at the rehearsal. But I guess not."

Brad stared into my gaze, and lifted a hand to brush a loose strand of hair behind my ear. He smiled softly, "I guess I'll have to stick to your side like caramel on an apple."

His comparison surprised a laugh out of me, and I grinned in return. It would not be a hardship to have this wonderful, charming, man at my side.

"You may want to anyway. Lindsey is Asher's cousin."

"I knew he looked familiar the other day." Brad sat back in his chair with a frown. "I never spent much time with her extended family since we were attending school out of state. They even have the same last name."

I saw Courtney smile out of the corner of my eye, and turned to look at her. Asher held her hand and lifted it up, the light caught just right on the large diamond causing it to sparkle even in the dim lighting. He kissed just above the ring.

A loud squeal blasted through the speakers as someone picked up the mic. All conversation stopped as everyone shifted to look at who had the mic. Samantha's hand on the mic shook as she glared at Courtney.

"This can't be good," Victoria muttered.

"I was going to do this tomorrow, but I can't stomach another minute of watching you two."

"Sam," Asher pleaded.

"I'm having your baby!" Samantha screeched. "And you're still going to marry her."

All the color faded out of Courtney's face, and she turned wide eyes to look at Asher. Samantha kept rambling into the mic, while Asher's family started yelling for an explanation from Asher. When Asher reached for Courtney's hand, she yanked it away and stood.

She took three steps before Asher grabbed her arm hard enough to stop her.

"Babe."

"Don't *Babe* me." She yanked her arm out of his grip and looked at Samantha. "How long?"

Sam smiled like an evil witch. "I've been seeing him since he proposed."

Courtney ripped her ring off, and slapped Asher hard enough for it to be heard through the room. "We're done."

She took off running out of the room, and Victoria ran after her. Asher tried to follow, but my dad was there to stop him.

"How dare you!" My dad yelled.

Asher's father joined them, and yelled at my father. "Don't yell at my son."

The yelling continued, and I watched my father's face

turn a concerning shade of purple. Brad rushed to his side just as my dad placed a hand on his chest. He looked at me, then collapsed. Brad caught him as he fell and lowered him to the floor on his back.

All the yelling around me sounded like it was coming from an echo chamber. I could only stare at my dying father as Brad checked for a pulse.

"Call 911!" Brad's instructions snapped me out of my daze.

I fumbled with my phone, and held my breath as it rang.

The dispatcher asked me a question, but I couldn't understand the words. A hand took the phone from me, and I didn't turn to see who, I could only stare as Brad performed CPR.

Time passed and I only stared. I only stopped staring when the paramedics arrived. They loaded my father on a stretcher and wheeled him away.

I tried to stand, but my legs kept me trapped in my chair. Brad hurried over to me, took one look, and grabbed the jacket on the back of my dad's chair to wrap around me.

"Beth, are you okay to go to the hospital with me?"

I nodded.

"Where's Victoria and Courtney?" he asked.

I looked around, but I had no idea.

"I'll call." I reached for my phone, but I no longer had it.

A young waitress held it out to me. "I'm sorry, I took over the call. You looked like you were going to faint."

Brad thanked her, and used my phone to call my family.

He took care of gathering their jackets and purses, and ushering me to his car.

"They'll meet us there." He told me.

The street lights blurred past me, and I could only see the agony on my father's face before he'd collapsed. The paramedics took him away from me, much like the paramedics had taken my mother ten years ago. She'd been too weak to fight to keep her heart beating after all the treatments.

We arrived at the hospital and Brad handed a frantic looking Victoria her purse so she could fill out the insurance paperwork. He found me a chair by Courtney.

I watched Victoria, the pain and worry on her face. Courtney wasn't much better, losing her fiancé and my dad in one night. Mascara ran down her cheeks, as she clutched my hand tight in hers. I could barely feel it.

"Do you want some water?" Brad asked Courtney and I.

His face held fear and worry for me. Fear like my dad had lived with daily while my mother fought for her life. Worry like Victoria felt now waiting for news about her second husband on death's door. I couldn't stand to see it.

"Go." I told him.

Confusion clouded his eyes. "Get water?"

"Just leave. I don't want to see you."

He looked stunned and hurt by my words. But it was better to hurt him now after only knowing him a couple weeks. He'd hurt so much more later. More if our relationship developed into something so much more. In a few short weeks he'd gone from stranger, to real dating when that hadn't been the deal. We couldn't have more, I couldn't risk more pain for either of us.

"I'm done."

"Beth—"

Victoria came over to us, interrupting whatever he'd been about to say. "They're moving us to another waiting room. I'm sorry Brad, but it's family only."

Brad's gaze pleaded with me as he said, "We'll talk later?"

"Thank you for helping my dad," I said, ignoring his plea.

I didn't look back as I walked away from him, I couldn't look at the hurt in his eyes any more. I followed Victoria, Courtney's hand still holding mine.

# Chapter Fourteen

Hours passed without news as I sat in the hard chair in the private waiting room reserved for the families of patients having heart surgery. The surgical team was doing everything they could. It was close to midnight when the doctor came out to see us.

She had a tired smile on her face. "The surgery was successful."

Relief washed over me and I didn't bother to listen to the rest of what she said.

"Can we see him?" Victoria asked.

"He's sedated. You can visit with him in the morning. We'll be monitoring him closely overnight."

Victoria handed her keys to Courtney, and sent both of us home. The ICU room my father was in only allowed one visitor overnight, and we needed to get a change of clothes to bring back for Victoria. As much as I hated it, it made more sense for me to get a few hours of sleep at home instead of trying to sleep on the uncomfortable chairs there.

In the car, Courtney didn't say a thing about Asher and

Samantha. She did try to get me to talk about why I ended it with Brad. But I just shook my head at her. My heart felt like it had been through a blender tonight, and I wanted to talk about it as much as she wanted to discuss her ruined wedding.

The next week passed in a blur of trips to and from the hospital. My dad grew stronger, and I spent as much time with him as I could. I hadn't even remembered about the flooring installation until Georgie called me. A frantic call to Sofie later, and she was using her emergency key and managing the flooring situation so I wouldn't have to spend any time away from the hospital while my dad was awake.

Brad called me multiple times over the weekend, but I'd ignored them all. Then the calls stopped, and I hadn't gotten any texts from him either. My mind was made up, but it hurt how easily he'd given up on me. It was a good thing I ended things when I did, I didn't want to think about how much it would hurt if we'd dated longer.

My dad looked at me as I checked my phone for the fifth time in ten minutes. "Go home, Beth."

"No, it's fine."

"I'm not going anywhere, Victoria will bring me my bland heart healthy lunch any minute. It'll be okay until you come back tomorrow."

His words piqued my curiosity.

"Did you know you had heart problems?"

He nodded. "I found out eight years ago."

The hurt stung as much as the questions that started spinning. "Why didn't you tell me?"

"I saw what seeing your mom's fight did to you. I

couldn't stand it if you looked at me with that same fearful expression every time you looked at me."

"We could have ran together. I would have helped you be healthier. I smuggled all those treats into the house for you, so you wouldn't have to eat Victoria's cooking."

He laughed. "Victoria wasn't keeping me under lock and key, forcing me to eat only what she wanted. We decided long ago to make healthier food choices."

I loved him with my entire soul, but I didn't know what to do with the bombshell he'd just dumped on me. All these years I'd painted Victoria as this horribly controlling step-monster, and she was simply feeding him the food that was good for his heart. She was helping him be healthier so he could keep this secret from me.

My phone beeped.

*Sofie: Floor done. Need help arranging the new furniture?*

*Me: Yes please.*

"My flooring is done. I need to go take a look at it." I gave him a gentle hug and kiss on his cheek.

"Do me a favor Beth, don't let fear stop you from living."

"I'll be back after the run tomorrow."

Sofie and Courtney spent three hours helping me fill my cabinets, and rearrange my new couch and chairs. Courtney had a great eye for tying a room together with little accents in the décor. Sofie and I sweated as we moved the furniture to where Courtney pointed. My sister had brought my suitcases over to my house when I called her about having a girls night at my place tonight.

We'd opted for Chinese take out instead of the typical

pizza, but I was content to sit on my new couch while Sofie and Courtney fought over the movie.

"When did you turn so feisty?" Sofie asked.

Courtney shrugged. "When I decided I am worth more."

Sofie smiled. "I'm so glad you aren't really a mean girl."

"Me too," I added. "You just needed to get rid of Asher."

"I wish my credit card debt was as easy to get rid of. I'm going to be paying for the wedding I never had for years."

Sofie gasped. "He won't help with the bills?"

Courtney shook her head. "He's saving for the baby."

My doorbell rang, and I looked at Sofie and Courtney questioningly, but they gave me confused shrugs. I got up from the couch and went to answer the door. I opened the door to find my boss with a box of 24 decadent chocolates, and a plate with sandwiches made by none other than his personal chef.

"Give me!" I reached for the chocolates.

He pulled them out of reach. "Aren't you going to invite me in?"

I stepped back and opened the door wider. He whistled at the sight of my new floor and furniture. As he walked by me to get a better look at the kitchen, I snatched the chocolates and closed the door. I rushed to the couch, letting Sebastian give himself a tour of the changes without me. He'd follow at his own pace.

"You know those chocolates are in trade for details of your dating life right?"

Sofie cringed hard, and Courtney shook her head vehemently.

Sebastian grimaced. "What did I just put my foot in?"

Sofie glared. "We're not talking about Brad Charmaine in this house until Beth wants to tell us why she dumped him."

Sebastian's head whipped towards me. "Brad? You didn't tell me it was Brad. I play poker with him and some other buddies."

I peeled the clear plastic wrap off the box of chocolates. "Doesn't matter, it's over. Never would have worked anyway."

Sebastian watched me as I stuffed my face with the chocolates in hope I wouldn't feel like crying. They were as good as I remembered. They melted so smoothly on my tongue, their creaminess contrasting with the bursts of raspberry filling. They all looked at me with concern, and I couldn't ignore their stares any longer.

"We were just fake dating anyway."

"What?!" Courtney and Sebastian said in unison.

I waved a hand towards Sofie to explain as I continued to eat the chocolate like my life depended on it. I'd finished the box by the time she finished going over the arrangement. She'd left out the part about dating for real, and I realized I hadn't told her that part before we'd broken up.

Courtney raised a hand, "Let me get this straight. All your feelings were fake."

"Just cosplaying." I got up to throw the box away.

A gleam appeared in Sebastian's clever gaze as he followed me into the kitchen with the plate of sandwiches. "So you wouldn't mind if Lindsey dances with him at the ball?"

Raging jealousy flared in me, and I took a minute to

tamp it down before responding. "He's free to dance with whoever he wants."

"I don't believe you."

"What do you want me to say Sebastian? That I'm a coward and I got scared? That I couldn't handle the thought of loving someone so much that it would break me to lose them?"

"I want you to be honest with yourself, and it sounds like you just were."

His phone rang, and he pulled it out of his pocket to silence it. He set the sandwiches on the counter.

"Thanks for the food." I grabbed the plate and put it in the fridge for lunch tomorrow.

He put his phone away. *"Fear is all you that stands between you and a brighter future."*

"Don't you dare use Ice Princess quotes to manipulate me."

"Do you know why I love comics so much?" He asked.

I shook my head.

"Because they teach that we can overcome even the scariest things if we are willing to try." He hugged me gently. "Think about that. I gotta run to poker night with the guys."

Sebastian left, and I poked at my spicy pork while my favorite superhero movie played on the TV. I knew that Sofie and Courtney were concerned about me, when they didn't pick the romance movie. My dad's words and Sebastian's circled, making me feel worse about what I'd done.

But it was too late now. Brad clearly didn't feel the same for me as I did for him. He would have tried harder to get me to talk to him.

# 

Chapter Fifteen

Marie smiled at me as soon as I walked up to the check in table for the race. "This is the biggest number of sign ups I've ever had."

"I'm so happy to hear that."

I was happy to hear it, but the drop of happiness didn't offset the misery I was currently drowning in. All night I'd tossed and turned at the thought of running into Brad this morning.

When my alarm went off, I'd hit snooze so many times I'd barely had enough time to grab my comic sneakers for the run. They'd been customized by a seller online for me. I'd left my tortoise costume at home since I'd run out of time. Instead I wore my normal running leggings and a shirt with the Ice Princess on it.

Marie looked behind me. "Where's Brad?"

"Being a coward."

I spun, and found Kim behind me.

She crossed her arms. "He's been eating donuts at my house all week. Even Zoey has gotten tired of it."

I fidgeted under her glare.

"Fix it." She pulled out a black prepaid plastic card, and held it out to me. "This is for the ball."

Stepping back I held my hands up. "I don't understand."

"He wants me to pay for him at the auction. My mother would never let me win, she's set him up to play a part in her charade." Kim grabbed my hand and put the card in it. "It'll either be you, or Lindsey that wins him. I'd much rather it be you."

She walked away and I just kept staring at the black card in my hand. A small sticky note on the back listed a dollar amount that made me gasp. He'd put ten thousand on the card.

Marie gently shook my shoulder. "I don't understand what that was all about, but I don't think you should be running today."

I nodded and she guided me to a chair behind the table to sit down. It wasn't until well after the craziness of getting the race started was done, that Marie had time to sit by me. She'd kept an eye on me while she'd checked in the racers, but left to give her annual inspirational speech.

When she returned, she patted my knee. I finally stopped staring at the card in my hand.

"Want to tell me about it?" she asked.

I started talking, and the words kept coming out. Tears streamed down my face when I told her my fears. There were so many things to be afraid of. I could get sick, he could get sick. We could spend all this time together and what was the point.

Marie patted my knee again, and handed me a tiny package of tissues to wipe my nose.

"I'm guessing you haven't been paying attention to my speeches."

"Huh?"

"Storms are wonderfully terrible things. Wonderful because it brings the rain that's needed for new life. Terrible because it can be so destructive and there's nothing that can be done. Death is hard, helplessly watching a sickness ravage your loved ones is terrible. But the terrible things in life don't mean we shouldn't live life. I never would have met you if I'd done that and that would be a very sad thing. Don't make life more sad, by hiding from the sunshine."

I drove in a daze to my dad's house while I thought about what Marie said. Courtney was the only one home when I walked inside the kitchen. She'd moved home to save money after quitting her job so she wouldn't have to see Samantha every day.

"Everything okay?" she asked. "I thought the big run was today."

"It was. I just needed to do something more important."

"Can I help?" She asked.

"Do you know where I can get a fancy mask fit for a princess?"

She hugged me and excitedly squealed so loud. I thought my ear drum would burst. She ran off to make calls, and I pulled the princess gown from my old room. An idea began to take form.

Cinderella wasn't fighting for her prince when she went to the ball. But I would be, and I wasn't going to lose my prince. I got my older sewing machine out of the closet, grabbed some scissors and got to work. I sent Courtney on a quest to the fabric and craft stores to pick up some things for me.

All day and the next I worked on my dress. I burned my fingers on hot glue and pricked myself stitching icicle decorations and various shades of iridescent organza fabric together. But as the sun set Saturday night, I grinned. My gown was fit for an Ice princess.

It shimmered as I spun, and Sofie applauded at the effect of sparkling snowflakes cascading down my sleeves.

So far, Courtney had struck out on finding me a mask that would work for the dress. The costume stores were out of masks as well since so many people had gotten them for the masquerade.

My time was running out, the ball had already started.

"What if you wrapped some of that shiny fabric around your head like a belt?" Sofie suggested. "Cut a couple holes for your eyes and boom, done."

Courtney looked horrified. "She'd ruin her hair and makeup."

While I'd been finishing up the final details, Courtney had been painstakingly curling ringlets in my hair. She'd even used diamond decorated bobby pins to secure half of them up. I don't know how she did the magic make up so quickly, but I loved how it enhanced my eyes. All the times she'd spent practicing her wedding look were benefiting me now.

"What are you ladies arguing about?" Victoria stood in the doorway of my room. She looked tired from all the days she'd been spending at the hospital with my Dad.

"I need a mask for the ball."

Victoria looked me up and down. "I have just the thing."

She returned a few minutes later with a small brown paper box filled with tissue paper. Nestled inside of it was a delicate blown glass mask adorned with white beads and silver swirls. A black ribbon extended from either side to tie it securely on my head. I was afraid to touch it since the mask itself was so thin and looked like it wouldn't take much to break it.

"Where did you get that?" Courtney asked.

Victoria smiled, "From Venice when I was younger."

"I can't wear that."

"I insist." Victoria took the mask out of the box and expertly tied it into place without disturbing all the pins.

As I stared at my reflection, I sucked in a breath and stared, awestruck at myself. The glass had a slight shimmer that made my skin underneath look like ice sparkling in the moonlight. The beads and swirls appeared to be a result of whatever magic that had transformed me.

Sofie jumped up from where she'd been sitting on my old bed. "Time to go. The website says the bid for Brad will be up soon."

I hugged Victoria, "Thank you."

When the hug was over, she dabbed at the corner of her

eye. "Go, win your doctor. I need some good news to share with your father."

The Town Hall was packed with cars and people. Sofie and Courtney tried to drop me off right in front of the door, but there was a line of cars wrapped around the block leading to the ball. I clutched the card from Kim in one hand.

"Run!" Sofie shouted, and she hopped out of the stopped car to open my door. "He's up next."

I waved at them, lifted the front of my dress, and took off running. The dress weighed me down as I ran, by the time I reached the ballroom I was out of breath.

I looked at the stage, where Brad stood in the spotlight. The line of remaining bachelors in the shadows behind him. He was wearing the prince costume from Marie, and it made me grin.

"Five thousand. Going once." The auctioneer rattled into the microphone. "Going twice."

A second spotlight shined onto the crowded floor where Lindsey stood, mask in hand smiling up at Brad like a cat that had gotten the canary.

"Ten thousand!" I shouted.

The auctioneer's jaw dropped, as did those closest around me. The spotlight searched through the crowd for me, and I started walking towards the stage. The crowd parted before me, and the light found me.

The auctioneer still stared, and I began to worry that I'd done something wrong. A bachelor from the shadows rushed the auctioneer, took the gavel, and slammed it on the podium.

A familiar voice yelled into the mic, "Sold, to the Ice Princess!"

I glanced at the podium briefly to confirm that it was indeed Sebastian. The auctioneer recovered, faster than I thought possible, and counted to three before declaring me the winner.

Brad looked stunned, as I stopped before the stage. Sebastian walked over to him and gave him a nudge. The crowd laughed, but I held my breath as I waited for Brad to do something, say something. Sebastian leaned close and spoke into his ear.

Then Brad was grinning, and hurrying towards me. He didn't even bother with finding the stairs, simply jumped off the stage to stand beside me.

In all of my preparations for this moment, I hadn't prepared what I'd say to him. But that didn't seem to matter. He pulled me close to him, and then we were kissing. Kissing while cheers went up in the crowd and the spotlight continued to shine. But I didn't care. I only cared that I hadn't been too late, that he hadn't run away, and that I was in his arms.

The spotlight faded, and the auction continued around us. But I knew in his arms that what we had wouldn't fade. I carefully pulled my mask free. I didn't need the mask of fear to protect my heart any longer. I was done hiding.

The Ice Princess had said it best. *Fear is all you that stands between you and a brighter future.*

I'd found my brighter future, and I wasn't going to hide from the sun.

# Epilogue

One year later, on a crisp October morning, Brad and I ran side by side through the park where I'd first met him. The cosplay run was being held here this year, and I couldn't have been happier. I smiled as I thought of all the things we'd done together since then.

Facing my fear was hard, but this right here, what I had with him was worth it. We'd talked for a long time after the masquerade about why I'd broken up with him.

Brad had attended his first comic convention ever with me, and I'd learned how to play cards from him. Sebastian had insisted on authentic whist games at the Regency Convention held at his estate. He'd been talking about a Tolkien convention, but I think that was due to Sofie's battle with the Book Beast.

"Ah!" Brad yelled, and fell.

I stopped running and looked behind me to see him on the ground next to a bush.

"Do you need a medic?" I frantically looked around to see if one would magically appear. There was no one.

He got to his knees, well, one knee. He reached down by his ankle, and I realized he must have twisted it. I rushed towards him to help him to the bench. But when I reached for his hand, he was holding something up instead.

Nestled in a black velvet box glinted a shiny diamond ring.

"Bethany Spencer, will you marry me?" he asked.

Words failed me as emotion overwhelmed me. I began nodding. I nodded until my vocal chords started working and I could speak.

"Yes!"

Cheering from the trees sounded, and I saw our family and friends surrounding us. My dad grinned, and I was happy to know he'd be with us for a long time yet. Zoey jumped up and down in her tiny Ice Princess costume, modeled after the one I'd worn to the ball. Even his mother smiled at us. She'd come around when she realized how much I meant to Brad.

Sebastian grinned slyly at Sofie, and I wondered if a ring was in her near future too.

Brad slipped the ring on my finger, then lifted me and twirled so fast I had to hold on.

I'd found my Prince Charming, and I would hold onto him forever.

## Apple Tree Kisses

The long beep blared from the washer, loud enough that I heard it from the kitchen over the pop-rock blasting from my phone. I put down the knife on the pink cutting board, next to the apple I'd finished slicing for mine and Zoey's snack. She'd insisted on having apples before our trip to the apple orchard today. Her second grade class had been learning about growing things, and Zoey had picked the trip for our Saturday mommy daughter date. The washer beeped again to remind me I could switch the whites to the dryer.

I glanced at the clock on the microwave to check the time. Forty minutes before we needed to leave to reach the orchard in time for our tour. Plenty of time to switch the laundry, take out the trash, and finish prepping our morning snack.

Zoey was supposed to be getting dressed and brushing her hair. Our morning routine was simple, Zoey helped with starting a load of laundry while I prepared breakfast. By the time we ate and got ready for the day the washer would be done. Then while Zoey got ready I switched the clothes to the dryer so they'd be ready to be put away when we got home later. At least that was the morning routine I tried to follow each day. More mornings than not, nothing went to plan and I was lucky to have her fed and hair brushed before dropping her off at school.

I pulled open the lid to the old washing machine before pulling out the first wet shirt. My heart sank as I took in the pink hue of what was supposed to be the white button-up shirt that I wore to work. A look into the washer revealed the rest of the clothes had also turned pink. I searched through the wet laundry before I found the culprit. A red stuffed toy in the shape of a heart. I got it for her for Valentine's Day last month.

"Mom!" Zoey called from upstairs.

I grabbed the toy, set it to the side, and quickly went through the process of adding bleach and starting the washer again. It wasn't the first time Zoey had slipped a toy into the wash and caused a color mishap.

"Mom!" Zoey said, closer this time.

She stood in the kitchen with a brush in one hand and hair ties in the other. I pointed at the chair at the kitchen island, and she climbed on top of it and held up the brush for me to help with her hair.

"What are we doing today?" I asked as I ran the brush through her chestnut brown hair.

"I want a braid."

The brush caught in her hair as I ran it through.

"Do birds sleep in your hair?" I teased Zoey. "I think they made a nest in it."

She shook her head, and I had to start brushing all over.

"Mom, can I have a puppy?"

"I thought you wanted a unicorn?"

"Ben has a puppy. Anna has a cat. Tyler has a fish. My whole class has pets, and I want one."

"Who would watch the puppy while you're at school and I'm at work?"

Her little shoulders slumped, and I finished tying off the braid. My heart broke for her, it wasn't fair, but I was supplying the best I could for her. Being a single parent wasn't easy, and there were too many things Zoey missed out on. I'd been chatting with a coworker about her new husky and a dog seemed like too much work.

I hugged her from behind and kissed her gently on the top of her head.

"How does learning to ride a horse sound?"

Zoey squealed, and her head snapped up, nailing me in the chin. I dropped my arms from around her, and rubbed where she'd bonked me.

Her eyes sparkled with hope as she looked up at me, "Really?"

"I'm getting a bonus from work, so I thought we could see how much the lessons were on our tour today."

She jumped up and down.

"Go grab your jacket, I'm going to take the trash out real quick."

I hugged Zoey again, and she ran upstairs towards her room. A few minutes later I had the apple slices into a container for the drive to the orchard. Zoey would be hungry well before we got there, and I hoped that with the little bit of peanut butter I'd added it would hold us both over until lunch.

As I took the garbage out, I saw the house next door had a rented moving truck in the driveway. The sound of dogs yipping had me turning to find Mr. and Mrs. Stanley walking their two Pomeranians, Teddy and Bear.

I smiled while greeting them. Mr. Stanley had his thinning white hair combed over, while his wife had hers curled around her face. The two had become surrogate grandparents to Zoey when I'd moved into the neighborhood. She'd be sad she wasn't out to see them or pet their dogs.

Mrs. Stanley handed her leash to Mr. Stanley so she could hug me. When she stepped back she excitedly chatted away.

"The Smith's rented that house out for the next six months. Paula told me that he's a handsome single young man."

Mr. Stanley clucked his tongue affectionately, "Don't be match-making. Let the young people match themselves."

It certainly wasn't the first time Mrs. Stanley had told me about eligible men in the area. It definitely wouldn't be the last. Mrs. Stanley seemed to have a rolodex somewhere with men she'd mentioned. Last spring I'd been home working in the flower bed by the front door and she'd even sent over a lawn guy that had been in the neighborhood advertising his company's landscape services. She was disappointed when her attempted set-up had only resulted in my helping him set up his website in exchange for four lawn treatments last year.

Zoey ran by me and both Pomeranians eagerly jumped up on her to lick her hands as she pet them both. She giggled, and soon the rest of us were too. After a bit, the

Stanley's left to continue their walk, the subject of the new neighbor dropped.

I grabbed my phone and keys while Zoey washed her hands. Twenty minutes later we were on our way, and I was glad we had extra time for the drive. Crestfield wasn't a busy town, but weekends brought tourists in. The Double-G Orchard was about thirty minutes outside of town and I wanted to enjoy the scenic drive through the tree-covered hills to get there.

I glanced in the rearview mirror to see Zoey frowning at the stuffed toy zebra in her hand.

"Everything okay, Zoey?" I asked. "We'll be at the orchard soon."

Zoey cleared her throat. She'd been doing that a lot more lately when she wanted to be treated like a grown up. I wasn't ready for her to get bigger, but she kept growing anyway.

"Did Daddy like apples?"

My heart lurched at the mention of Zane, seven years had dulled the freshness of his passing but there was still a gaping hole in my heart for what our life together should have been.

"He sure did Baby. He would eat an apple everyday to keep the doctor away."

She wrinkled her nose. "Why would Daddy want to keep Uncle Brad away?"

I laughed, since the only doctor Zoey knew was my brother since he did her check-ups. "It's just something people say. Apples are healthy and if you're healthy you don't need a doctor. Uncle Brad would much rather see us healthy than sick."

"Is Uncle Brad coming over for dinner?" Zoey asked.

"Him and Beth."

Zoey squeaked in delight and started whispering to her zebra conspiratorially. I turned my attention back to the road, letting my thoughts drift to what should have been. Zane should have come home from deployment, he should have been able to meet his daughter. He should be in the car with us on a family outing and Zoey should have a sibling to whisper to instead of a stuffed toy. But he wasn't, and I had to be enough for both the parents that she deserved.

I wished for a much different life for Zoey. Filled with family. I had my brother Brad to help out after our mother had disowned me. Luckily for me and Zoey his fiancé Beth was the best aunt a seven year old could ask for. Beth and Brad loved Zoey so much I had to keep reminding them both that they needed to stop spoiling her rotten.

The drive was filled with Zoey's happy chatter to her zebra and the music on the radio. I smiled at the beauty of the hills covered in trees, and little yellow flowers starting to bloom. Spring had truly arrived and was in full swing. I was glad for the cold days to be behind us, and welcomed the sunshine being out in force.

We arrived at the orchard and drove under the metal archway stating "Double-G Orchard". I parked the car, and heard the click of Zoey's seatbelt a second later.

"Hold on Zippy!" I turned to see her with one hand holding her zebra and the other on the door handle about to get out. "Snack first, and your zebra stays in the car."

She pouted, and her bottom lip quivered. "Mom! Her name is Zoey-Zebra now. "

I suppressed the urge to smile at the name she'd picked

for her stuffed toy. "You know the deal. Toys stay in the car so we don't lose them. You don't want a goat to eat Zoey-Zebra do you?"

She continued to pout as she arranged her toy next to her booster seat and I pulled the apple slices from earlier out.

"How many do I have to eat?" Zoey asked.

I looked at the clock to see we had ten minutes before the tour. "Let's see how many we can make disappear in five minutes."

Zoey ate more peanut butter than apples, but I didn't care so long as she ate something. She was the pickiest eater, and due for a growth spurt any day. We used wet wipes from my purse to get the sticky apple juice off our fingers and we only had five minutes before it would be time for the tour.

The ticket booth attendant, a teenage girl more interested in texting than in confirming our reservation, gave us two bright blue, paper wristbands. I was disappointed when I didn't see a sign about horse riding lessons, and I didn't want Zoey to hear me ask. Maybe there'd be a sign or something when we got to the petting zoo part of the tour.

There weren't many people walking about, but a group of three stood under the sign for the next tour. They were busy chatting and putting their own blue wristbands on. I guided Zoey towards them and hoped we were in the right spot.

Two of the other three for the tour were old enough to be Zoey's grandparents, and the third I guessed was their grandson. The grandmother kept smoothing the boy's dark hair down as they talked happily about the petting zoo at the end of the tour. I no longer counted how frequently I wished for grandparents that would love and care for Zoey. My grandparents had passed when I was in high school and my own mother wasn't the motherly type, let alone the type of person someone would hope to have for a grandmother. The few times we'd ran into each other since Zoey was born she'd pretended we didn't exist.

I smiled at the older woman when she looked my way. Zoey immediately started talking to the boy, who introduced himself as Rocky, asking if there would be a zebra in the petting zoo. She'd read all about them in her library book and I made a mental note of taking her to the zoo in the big city before she lost interest.

"Howdy folks!"

I looked up to see an older gentleman wearing striped overalls and a straw hat. His face was wrinkled from a life well lived, the smile lines were deepest. He looked familiar, but that probably meant I'd seen him around town at some point. Crestfield was big enough to keep running into the people, but not so small that I knew everyone. Growing up, Mother made sure Brad and I only associated with those she approved of in her social circle. Now I only remembered the names of people if they were someone at Zoey's school, doctor's office, or a client of mine.

"I'm Grady of the Double-G Orchard. Is everyone ready to see some trees?" He waved a hand to two big black horses hooked up to a flatbed trailer.

Zoey jumped up and down and squeezed my hand as she pointed at the horses. Another man, nearer my age, stood between the bulky horses holding the reins in a gloved hand. The cut of his jeans and what I could see of his shoulders under a dark green shirt was enough to make me curious about what the rest of him looked like. I couldn't quite get a good look at his face due to the angle of his black cowboy hat.

Grady guided us to the trailer and lowered a step attached to the side of the trailer that would make it easier for us to get in. Benches padded by quilts were lined up in rows for us to sit on. The blankets looked worn, with the dark blue denim sun-bleached to a lighter shade. After Zoey and I sat down on the second bench behind the others, I ran a hand over the red stitches. The embroidered flowers were beautiful and imperfect. There were spots where the stitches didn't quite follow the same line, and the stitches were close to the same size, but not. Someone had spent a lot of time covering the quilt in a hand-stitched flower and leaf pattern.

"My wife Grace made those blankets," Grady said from the front of the trailer. "She's the better half of the double G."

I looked up to see him smiling at his joke. He'd taken a seat on a bench situated at the front of the trailer. He took the horse reins from the other man. Then, like something out of an old western, Grady clicked his tongue and the horses began pulling the trailer forward.

The morning sun warmed my skin, and I enjoyed the gentle breeze as it moved through my hair. I'd left it down today since I'd forgotten to pull it up after talking to the Stanleys. I closed my eyes to take in the moment. No doubt if Mrs. Stanley was here she'd already be handing me that cowboy's number. Or giving him mine, she hadn't tried setting me up with a cowboy yet.

Shade fell over my eyes and I opened them to see we'd entered the blossom-covered orchard. Tiny white and pink flowers covered the trees. Bees buzzed around us, and I half expected to see the trees shaking as a result.

Rocky turned to his grandpa, "It sounds like your razor."

His grandmother smiled, while his grandpa laughed in response.

Zoey tapped my shoulder. "Razors don't make a sound."

The boy glared at Zoey. "They do too. My dad's and grandpa's do."

She'd only ever seen the plastic disposable kind that I used to shave my legs. She'd never seen the electric kind since I didn't use one.

I sighed and told both of them, "There are some that do, and some that don't."

As we went through the apple trees, Grady told them about the different varieties. Golden delicious, Honeycrisp, Pink Lady's, and three others I wasn't familiar with. Each of the apples sounded delicious, with some ripening in August instead of November and I mentally made a note to come back in the fall so we could try some.

The conversation shifted to the work his wife put into the orchard right beside him. They'd started off small, leasing land until they'd saved enough to buy. Starting with the fruit trees and a couple of working horses. As their kids grew older, they'd expanded into beekeeping, and pumpkin patches. The petting zoo developed when his daughter kept talking them into keeping the strays she brought home. Pride shined through him as he spoke of his kids.

"Grace's had to slow down recently, but she's still the same fire cracker I fell in love with."

The older woman chuckled, "It must have taken her a long time to make these quilts. Does she sell them? The embroidery is beautiful."

Grady's grin grew. "She'll be pleased to know someone noticed the stitches. Those blankets are made out of the jeans worn out here. When they couldn't be patched any longer, she used the pieces that were still good for the pieces in her quilts. Here at the Double-G Orchard we don't waste."

"And the leaf pattern?" I asked. "It's beautiful."

"She doodled it herself." He guided the horses out of the orchard.

The sun shone bright overhead now that we were out of the trees. We were surrounded by a pasture covered in spring grass.

I looked down at the stitching once more, there were so many different types of leaves connected by a swirling vine. Nothing wasted. I looked at Zoey, in her blue princess sneakers, sparkly blue jeans, and purple jacket. She was still outgrowing her clothes faster than I could get her new ones. I couldn't imagine keeping up with her and having time to quilt as well.

Zoey gasped, "Mom! I want a horse like that one!"

I looked to where she pointed, the cowboy from before was on top of a beautiful horse. If I'd thought my glimpse of him earlier was enough to swoon over, I was glad to be sitting down now. It'd been a long time since I'd seen a man that was handsome enough for me to take notice of. Short dark hair lined his jaw, and he moved as if he was in tune with his horse. The horse's mane and tail were a dark black, while the body of the horse was a reddish brown. The man and horse trotted gracefully along the fence line. Without pulling the reins the horse seemed to know when it needed to stop or move along.

Grady cleared his throat, "Afraid that horse isn't for sale Ma'am. My son would have my hide if I tried to sell his prized bay."

"He's beautiful," I said to Grady, then turned to Zoey. "Honey, we don't have any place to keep a horse."

The older woman giggled. "I bet she has her Dad wrapped around her little finger."

"My Daddy died," Zoey said matter of factly.

The woman's jaw dropped and she sputtered as she looked at me. Her face was full of embarrassed horror. "I'm so sorry."

I did my best not to flinch, and instead nodded my head. "It was a long time ago."

I hated receiving condolences, I'd had my fill of them over the years. Many people reacted the same as this woman when they found out. Zoey's blunt delivery didn't help much either.

The boy with the older couple, then looked at Zoey. "You can have my Dad."

Zoey looked like she was considering it while the couple chuckled.

The grandpa ruffled the boy's hair, "Your Momma would probably have an issue with that."

Before Zoey had replied to the boy, the cowboy took off at a gallop across the field. She grinned as big as her face would allow as she watched the horse run. I thanked the sky above the subject of dads dropped.

An hour later, we'd been taken past the fields of alfalfa and another pasture where half a dozen horses roamed free. We arrived at a classic red barn with a small corral and got off the trailer. The pen was filled with fuzzy animals. Goats and bunnies scampered around the corral, while a llama, lambs, and pigs were in separate pens nearby.

"Welcome to Gabby's Petting zoo." Grady waved his daughter over to where we stood by the gate.

Gabby had gorgeous curly auburn hair in a ponytail, and a bright smile that looked familiar. A straw sun hat hung from the string around her neck. She wore striped overalls similar to her father. Though hers were tucked into muck covered boots, while Grady's didn't have much dirt on them.

She proceeded to tell us the rules for petting the animals, reminding us to be calm, and making sure we used sanitizer before touching them. I stood close to Zoey as she pet a fat gray bunny. A smaller black rabbit hopped around the pen and proceeded to head-butt a brown bunny in the ribs.

"Is that normal?" I asked Gabby.

She laughed. "That's our jackalope."

"Jackalope's aren't real!" Zoey declared.

Gabby winked. "Don't tell Jack that. He learned that from one of the rams in the other pen."

I laughed this time.

"Sorry if I'm nosy. . ." Gabby said. "You look familiar. Do I know you?"

# Afterword

Thank you so much for picking up Masquerading with Dr. Charming! I've always loved the story of Cinderella and her Prince. I learned from her to step out of my comfort zone to pursue dreams. I hope I did her story justice in this modern day retelling.

I was privileged to write this story about a health care hero. I'm so grateful for the tireless efforts of the medical professionals. There's a special soft spot in my heart for my family and friends in this field that have gone through so many hours during 2020 and 2021 helping those they care for.

Just a quick comment about reviews. I'm grateful for each comment that is left on my books. It's incredibly gratifying when someone says they enjoy my book. On the tough days those comments help me to keep writing. Honest reviews also help bring the attention of other readers. If you have a minute to spare, and liked this book, please leave a review.

Cellier's *Voice of Power*, and Shannon Hale's *The Goose Girl* will love the strong-willed protagonist, talking animals, and the intrigue of breaking a curse.

**Elemental Heir:**

The Bride Trials

**BIO:**

Jessica Parker has always had her nose in book. Her book affair began with fairy tales and dreams for finding her true love. While she found a few frogs during her search, she is happy to report that her dashing prince swept her off her feet and they are living happily ever after.

At home you can find Jessica with a dog by her feet and book in her hand. Otherwise check the water because she's an avid scuba diver. Her experiences on land and sea have resulted in a never ending list of stories to be written.

To stay caught up on her books about love and magic join her newsletter or follow her at:

https://jessicaparkerstories.com/

https://www.facebook.com/JessicaParkerStories/

www.ingramcontent.com/pod-product-compliance
Lightning Source LLC
Chambersburg PA
CBHW021546150726
47990CB00006B/2421